WHERE WORLDS MEET.

BY

HENRYK SIENKIEWICZ,

Author of "Quo Vadis," "Children of the Soil," "Dust and Ashes,"
"The New Soldier," "Her Tragic Fate," etc.

TRANSLATED BY
J CHRISTIAN BAY.

Fredonia Books
Amsterdam. The Netherlands

Where Worlds Meet

by
Henryk Sienkiewicz

ISBN: 1-58963-329-6

Reprinted from the 1899 edition

Fredonia Books
Amsterdam, The Netherlands
http://www.fredoniabooks.com

In order to make original editions of historical works
available to scholars at an economical price, this
facsimile of the original edition of 1899 is
reproduced from the best available copy and has
been digitally enhanced to improve legibility, but the
text remains unaltered to retain historical
authenticity.

INTRODUCTION.

HENRYK SIENKIEWICZ.

I once read a short story, in which a Slav author had all the lilies and bells in a forest bending toward each other, whispering and resounding softly the words: "Glory! Glory! Glory!" until the whole forest and then the whole world repeated the song of flowers.

Such is to-day the fate of the author of the powerful historical trilogy: "With Fire and Sword," "The Deluge" and "Pan Michael," preceded by short stories, "Lillian Morris," "Yanko the Musician," "After Bread," "Hania," "Let Us Follow Him," followed by two problem novels, "Without Dogma," and "Children of the Soil," and crowned by a

masterpiece of an incomparable artistic beauty,
"Quo Vadis." Eleven good books adopted
from the Polish language and set into circulation are of great importance for the English-
reading people—just now I am emphasizing
only this—because these books are written in
the most beautiful language ever written by
any Polish author! Eleven books of masterly,
personal, and simple prose! Eleven good
books given to the circulation and received not
only with admiration but with gratitude—
books where there are more or less good or
sincere pages, but where there is not one on
which original humor, nobleness, charm, some
comforting thoughts, some elevated sentiments do not shine. Some other author would
perhaps have stopped after producing "Quo
Vadis," without any doubt the best of Sienkiewicz's books. But Sienkiewicz looks into the
future and cares more about works which he is

going to write, than about those which we
have already in our libraries, and he renews
his talents, searching, perhaps unknowingly,
for new themes and tendencies.

When one knows how to read a book, then
from its pages the author's face looks out on
him, a face not material, but just the same
full of life. Sienkiewicz's face, looking on us
from his books, is not always the same; it
changes, and in his last book ("Quo Vadis")
it is quite different, almost new.

There are some people who throw down a
book after having read it, as one leaves a bot-
tle after having drank the wine from it.
There are others who read books with a pencil
in their hands, and they mark the most striking passages. Afterward, in the hours of rest,
in the moments when one needs a stimulant
from within and one searches for harmony,
sympathy of a thing apparently so dead and

strange as a book is, they come back to the
marked passages, to their own thoughts, more
comprehensible since an author expressed
them; to their own sentiments, stronger and
more natural since they found them in some-
body else's words.   Because ofttimes it seems
to us—the common readers—that there is no
difference between our interior world and the
horizon of great authors, and we flatter ourselves by believing that we are only less daring, less brave than are thinkers and poets,
that some interior lack of courage stopped us
from having formulated our impressions. And
in this sentiment there is a great deal of truth.
But while this expression of our thoughts
seems to us to be a daring, to the others it is
a need; they even do not suspect how much
they are daring and new.   They must, according to the words of a poet, "Spin out the love,
as the silkworm spins its web."   That is their

capital distinction from common mortals; we recognize them by it at once; and that is the reason we put them above the common level. On the pages of their books we find not the traces of the accidental, deeper penetrating into the life or more refined feelings, but the whole harvest of thoughts, impressions, dispositions, written skilfully, because studied deeply. We also leave something on these pages. Some people dry flowers on them, the others preserve reminiscences. In every one of Sienkiewicz's volumes people will deposit a great many personal impressions, part of their souls; in every one they will find them again after many years.

There are three periods in Sienkiewicz's literary life. In the first he wrote short stories, which are masterpieces of grace and ingenuity —at least some of them. In those stories the reader will meet frequent thoughts about general problems, deep observations of life—and notwithstanding his idealism, very truthful about spiritual moods, expressed with an easy and sincere hand. Speaking about Sienkiewicz's works, no matter how small it may be, one has always the feeling that one speaks about a known, living in general memory work. Almost every one of his stories is like a stone thrown in the midst of a flock of sparrows gathering in the winter time around barns: one throw arouses at once a flock of winged reminiscences.

The other characteristics of his stories are uncommonness of his conceptions, masterly compositions, ofttimes artificial. It happens also that a story has no plot ("From the Diary of a Tutor in Pozman," "Bartek the Victor"), no action, almost no matter ("Yamyol!"), but the reader is rewarded by simplicity, rural theme, humoristic pictures ("Comedy of Errors: A Sketch of American Life"), pity for the little and poor ("Yanko the Musician"), and those qualities make the reader remember his stories well. It is almost impossible to forget—under the general impressions—about his striking and standing-out figures ("The Lighthouse Keeper of Aspinwall"), about the individual impression they leave on our minds. Apparently they are commonplace, every-day people, but the author's talent puts on them an original individuality, a particular stamp, which makes one remember them forever and afterward apply them to the individuals which one meets in life. No matter how insignificant socially is the figure chosen by Sienkiewicz for his story, the great talent of the author magnifies its striking features, not seen by common people, and makes of it a masterpiece of literary art.

Although we have a popular saying: *Com-*

paraison n'est pas raison, one cannot refrain from stating here that this love for the poor, the little, and the oppressed, brought out so powerfully in Sienkiewicz's short stories, constitutes a link between him and François Coppée, who is so great a friend of the friendless and the oppressed, those who, without noise, bear the heaviest chains, the pariahs of our happy and smiling society. The only difference between the short stories of these two writers is this, that notwithstanding all the mastercraft of Coppée work, one forgets the impressions produced by the reading of his work—while it is almost impossible to forget "The Lighthouse Keeper" looking on any lighthouse, or "Yanko the Musician" listening to a poor wandering boy playing on the street, or "Bartek the Victor" seeing soldiers of which military discipline have made machines rather than thinking beings, or "The

Diary of a Tutor" contemplating the pale face of children overloaded with studies. Another difference between those two writers—the comparison is always between their short stories—is this, that while Sienkiewicz's figures and characters are universal, international—if one can use this adjective here—and can be applied to the students of any country, to the soldiers of any nation, to any wandering musician and to the light-keeper on any sea, the figures of François Coppée are mostly Parisian and could be hardly displaced from their Parisian surroundings and conditions.

Sometimes the whole short story is written for the sake of that which the French call *pointe*. When one has finished the reading of "Zeus's Sentence," for a moment the charming description of the evening and Athenian night is lost. And what a beautiful description it is! If the art of reading were cultivated in America as it is in France and Germany, I would not be surprised if some American Legouvé or Strakosch were to add to his répertoire such productions of prose as this humorously poetic "Zeus's Sentence," or that mystic madrigal, "Be Blessed."

"But the dusk did not last long," writes Sienkiewicz. "Soon from the Archipelago appeared the pale Selene and began to sail like a silvery boat in the heavenly space. And the walls of the Acropolis lighted again, but they beamed now with a pale green light, and looked more than ever like the vision of a dream."

But all these, and other equally charming pictures, disappear for a moment from the memory of the reader. There remains only the final joke—only Zeus's sentence. "A virtuous woman—especially when she loves another man—can resist Apollo. But surely and always a stupid woman will resist him."

Only when one thinks of the story does one see that the ending—that "immoral conclusion" I should say if I were not able to understand the joke—does not constitute the essence of the story. Only then we find a delight in the description of the city for which the wagons cater the divine barley, and the water is carried by the girls, "with amphoræ poised on their shoulders and lifted hands, going home, light and graceful, like immortal nymphs."

And then follow such paragraphs as the following, which determine the real value of the work:

"The voice of the God of Poetry sounded so beautiful that it performed a miracle. Behold! In the Ambrosian night the gold spear standing on the Acropolis of Athens trembled, and the marble head of the gigantic statue turned toward the Acropolis in order to hear better. . . . Heaven and earth listened to it; the sea stopped roaring and lay peacefully near the shores; even pale Selene stopped her night wandering in the sky and stood motionless over Athens."

"And when Apollo had finished, a light wind arose and carried the song through the whole of Greece, and wherever a child in the cradle heard only a tone of it, that child grew into a poet."

What poet? Famed by what song? Will he not perhaps be a lyric poet?

The same happens with "Lux in Tenebris." One reads again and again the description of the fall of the mist and the splashing of the rain dropping in the gutter, "the cawing of the crows, migrating to the city for their winter quarters, and, with flapping of wings, roosting in the trees." One feels that the

whole misery of the first ten pages was necessary in order to form a background for the
two pages of heavenly light, to bring out the
brightness of that light. "Those who have
lost their best beloved," writes Sienkiewicz,
"must hang their lives on something; otherwise they could not exist." In such sentences
—and it is not the prettiest, but the shortest
that I have quoted—resounds, however, the
quieting wisdom, the noble love of that art
which poor Kamionka "respected deeply and
was always sincere toward." During the long
years of his profession he never cheated nor
wronged it, neither for the sake of fame nor
money, nor for praise nor for criticism. He
always wrote as he felt. Were I not like Ruth
of the Bible, doomed to pick the ears of corn
instead of being myself a sower—if God had
not made me critic and worshipper but artist
and creator—I could not wish for another ne-

2

crology than those words of Sienkiewicz regarding the statuary Kamionka.

Quite another thing is the story "At the
Source." None of the stories except "Let Us
Follow Him" possess for me so many tran-
scendent beauties, although we are right to be
angry with the author for having wished, during the reading of several pages, to make us
believe an impossible thing—that he was de-
ceiving us. It is true that he has done it in a
masterly manner—it is true that he could not
have done otherwise, but at the same time
there is a fault in the conception, and although
Sienkiewicz has covered the precipice with
flowers, nevertheless the precipice exists.

On the other hand, it is true that one reading the novel will forget the trick of the author
and will see in it only the picture of an immense happiness and a hymn in the worship of
love. Perhaps the poor student is right when

he says: "Among all the sources of happiness, that from which I drank during the fever is the clearest and best." "A life which love has not visited, even in a dream, is still worse."

Love and faith in woman and art are two constantly recurring themes in "Lux in Tenebris," "At the Source," "Be Blessed," and "Organist of Ponikila."

When Sienkiewicz wrote "Let Us Follow Him," some critics cried angrily that he lessens his talent and moral worth of the literature; they regretted that he turned people into the false road of mysticism, long since left. Having found Christ on his pages, the least religious people have recollected how gigantic he is in the writings of Heine, walking over land and sea, carrying a red, burning sun instead of a heart. They all understood that to introduce Christ not only worthily or beautifully, but simply and in such a manner that we would not be obliged to turn away from the picture, would be a great art—almost a triumph.

In later times we have made many such attempts. "The Mysticism" became to-day an article of commerce. The religious tenderness and simplicity was spread among Parisian newspaper men, playwrights and novelists. Such as Armand Sylvèstre, such as Theodore de Wyzewa, are playing at writing up Christian dogmas and legends. And a strange thing! While the painters try to bring the Christ nearer to the crowd, while Fritz von Uhde or Lhermitte put the Christ in a country school, in a workingman's house, the weakling writers, imitating poets, dress Him in old, faded, traditional clothes and surround Him with a theatrical light which they dare to call "mysticism." They are crowding the porticos of the temple, but they are merely merchants.   Anatole France alone cannot be placed in the same crowd.

In "Let Us Follow Him" the situation and characters are known, and are already to be found in literature.   But never were they painted so simply, so modestly, without romantic complaints and exclamations.   In the first chapters of that story there appears an epic writer with whom we have for a long time been familiar.   We are accustomed to that uncommon simplicity.   But in order to appreciate the narrative regarding Antea, one must listen attentively to this slow prose and then one will notice the rhythmic sentences following one after the other.   Then one feels that the author is building a great foundation for the action.   Sometimes there occurs a brief, sharp sentence ending in a strong, short word, and the result is that Sienkiewicz has given us a masterpiece which justifies the en-

thusiasm of a critic, who called him a Prince
of Polish Prose.

In the second period of his literary activity,
Sienkiewicz has produced his remarkable historical trilogy, "The Deluge," "With Fire and
Sword," and "Pan Michael," in which his talent shines forth powerfully, and which possess
absolutely distinctive characters from his short
stories. The admirers of romanticism cannot
find any better books in historical fiction.
Some critic has said righteously about Sienkiewicz, speaking of his "Deluge," that he is
"the first of Polish novelists, past or present,
and second to none now living in England,
France, or Germany."

Sienkiewicz being himself a nobleman,
therefore naturally in his historical novels he
describes the glorious deeds of the Polish nobility, who, being located on the frontier of
such barbarous nations as Turks, Kozaks,

Tartars, and Wolochs (to-day Roumania), had defended Europe for centuries from the invasions of barbarism and gave the time to Germany, France, and England to outstrip Poland in the development of material welfare and general civilization among the masses— the nobility being always very refined— though in the fifteenth century the literature of Poland and her sister Bohemia (Chechy) was richer than any other European country, except Italy. One should at least always remember that Nicolaus Kopernicus (Kopernik) was a Pole and John Huss was a Chech.

Historical novels began in England, or rather in Scotland, by the genius of Walter Scott, followed in France by Alexandre Dumas *pere*. These two great writers had numerous followers and imitators in all countries, and every nation can point out some more or less successful writer in that field, but who

never attained the great success of Sienkiewicz, whose works are translated into many
languages, even into Russian, where the an-
tipathy for the Polish superior degree of civilization is still very eager.

The superiority of Sienkiewicz's talent is
then affirmed by this fact of translation, and I
would dare say that he is superior to the father
of this kind of novels, on account of his historical coloring, so much emphasized in Walter Scott. This important quality in the historical novel is truer and more lively in the
Polish writer, and then he possesses that psychological depth about which Walter Scott
never dreamed. Walter Scott never has created such an original and typical figure as Za-
globa is, who is a worthy rival to Shakespeare's Falstaff. As for the description of
duelings, fights, battles, Sienkiewicz's fantas-
tically heroic pen is without rival.

Alexandre Dumas, notwithstanding the biting criticism of Brunetière, will always remain a great favorite with the reading masses, who are searching in his books for pleasure, amusement, and distraction. Sienkiewicz's historical novels possess all the interesting qualities of Dumas, and besides that they are full of wholesome food for thinking minds. His colors are more shining, his brush is broader, his composition more artful, chiselled, finished, better built, and executed with more vigor. While Dumas amuses, pleases, distracts, Sienkiewicz astonishes, surprises, bewitches. All uneasy preoccupations, the dolorous echoes of eternal problems, which philosophical doubt imposes with the everlasting anguish of the human mind, the mystery of the origin, the enigma of destiny, the inexplicable necessity of suffering, the short, tragical, and sublime vision of the future of the soul, and the future not less difficult to be guessed of by the human race in this material world, the torments of human conscience and responsibility for the deeds, is said by Sienkiewicz without any pedanticism, without any dryness.

If we say that the great Hungarian author Maurice Jokai, who also writes historical novels, pales when compared with that fascinating Pole who leaves far behind him the late lions in the field of romanticism, Stanley J. Weyman and Anthony Hope, we are through with that part of Sienkiewicz's literary achievements.

In the third period Sienkiewicz is represented by two problem novels, "Without Dogma" and "Children of the Soil."

The charm of Sienkiewicz's psychological novels is the synthesis so seldom realized and as I have already said, the plastic beauty and abstract thoughts. He possesses also an admirable assurance of psychological analysis, a mastery in the painting of customs and characters, and the rarest and most precious faculty of animating his heroes with intense, personal life, which, though it is only an illusionary life appears less deceitful than the real life.

In that field of novels Sienkiewicz differs greatly from Balzac, for instance, who forced himself to paint the man in his perversity or in his stupidity. According to his views life is the racing after riches. The whole of Balzac's philosophy can be resumed in the deification of the force. All his heroes are "strong men" who disdain humanity and take advantage of it. Sienkiewicz's psychological novels are not lacking in the ideal in his conception of life; they are active powers, forming human souls. The reader finds there, in a well-balanced proportion, good and bad ideas of life, and he represents this life as a good thing, worthy of living.

He differs also from Paul Bourget, who as a German savant counts how many microbes are in a drop of spoiled blood, who is pleased with any ferment, who does not care for healthy souls, as a doctor does not care for healthy people—and who is fond of corruption. Sienkiewicz's analysis of life is not exclusively pathological, and we find in his novels healthy as well as sick people as in the real life. He takes colors from twilight and aurora to paint with, and by doing so he strengthens our energy, he stimulates our ability for thinking about those eternal problems, difficult to be decided, but which existed and will exist as long as humanity will exist.

He prefers green fields, the perfume of flowers, health, virtue, to Zola's liking for crime, sickness, cadaverous putridness, and manure.

He prefers *l' ame humaine* to *la bete humaine.*

He is never vulgar even when his heroes do not wear any gloves, and he has these common points with Shakespeare and Molière, that he does not paint only certain types of humanity, taken from one certain part of the country, as it is with the majority of French writers who do not go out of their dear Paris; in Sienkiewicz's novels one can find every kind of people, beginning with humble peasants and modest noblemen created by God, and ending with proud lords made by the kings.

In the novel "Without Dogma," there are many keen and sharp observations, said masterly and briefly; there are many states of the soul, if not always very deep, at least written with art. And his merit in that respect is greater than of any other writers, if we take in consideration that in Poland heroic lyricism and poetical picturesqueness prevail in the literature.

The one who wishes to find in the modern literature some aphorism to classify the characteristics of the people, in order to be able afterward to apply them to their fellow-men, must read "Children of the Soil."

But the one who is less selfish and wicked, and wishes to collect for his own use such a library as to be able at any moment to take a book from a shelf and find in it something which would make him thoughtful or would make him forget the ordinary life,—he must get "Quo Vadis," because there he will find pages which will recomfort him by their beauty and dignity; it will enable him to go out from his surroundings and enter into himself, *i. e.*, in that better man whom we sometimes feel in our interior. And while reading this book he ought to leave on its pages the traces of his readings, some marks made with a lead pencil or with his whole memory.

It seems that in that book a new man was aroused in Sienkiewicz, and any praise said about this unrivaled masterpiece will be as pale as any powerful lamp is pale comparatively with the glory of the sun. For instance. if I say that Sienkiewicz has made a thorough study of Nero's epoch, and that his great talent and his plastic imagination created the most powerful pictures in the historical background, will it not be a very tame praise, compared with his book—which, while reading it, one shivers and the blood freezes in one's veins?

In "Quo Vadis" the whole *alta Roma*, beginning with slaves carrying mosaics for their refined masters, and ending with patricians, who were so fond of beautiful things that one of them for instance used to kiss at every moment a superb vase, stands before our eyes as if it was reconstructed by a magical power from ruins and death.

There is no better description of the burning of Rome in any literature. While reading it everything turns red in one's eyes, and immense noises fill one's ears. And the moment when Christ appears on the hill to the frightened Peter, who is going to leave Rome, not feeling strong enough to fight with mighty Cæsar, will remain one of the strongest passages of the literature of the whole world.

After having read again and again this great—shall I say the greatest historical novel?—and having wondered at its deep conception, masterly execution, beautiful language, powerful painting of the epoch, plastic description of customs and habits, enthusiasm of the first followers of Christ, refinement of Roman civilization, corruption of the old world, the question rises: What is the dominating idea of the author, spread out all over the whole book? It is the cry of Christians murdered in circuses: *Pro Christo!*

Sienkiewicz searching always and continually for a tranquil harbor from the storms of conscience and investigation of the tormented mind, finds such a harbor in the religious sentiments, in lively Christian faith. This idea is woven as golden thread in a silk brocade, not only in "Quo Vadis," but also in all his novels. In "Fire and Sword" his principal hero is an outlaw; but all his crimes, not only against society, but also against nature, are redeemed by faith, and as a consequence of it afterward by good deeds. In the "Children of the Soul," he takes one of his principal characters upon one of seven Roman hills, and having displayed before him in the most eloquent way the might of the old Rome, the might as it

never existed before and perhaps never will
exist again, he says: "And from all that nothing is left only crosses! crosses! crosses!"   It
seems to us that in "Quo Vadis" Sienkiewicz
strained all his forces to reproduce from one
side all the power, all riches, all refinement, all
corruption of the Roman civilization in order
to get a better contrast with the great advantages of the cry of the living faith: *Pro
Christo!*   In that cry the asphyxiated not only
in old times but in our days also find refresh-
ment; the tormented by doubt, peace.   From
that cry flows hope, and naturally people pre-
fer those from whom the blessing comes to
those who curse and doom them.

Sienkiewicz considers the Christian faith as
the principal and even the only help which
humanity needs to bear cheerfully the burden
and struggle of every-day life.   Equally his
personal experience as well as his studies made

him worship Christ. He is not one of those who say that religion is good for the people at large. He does not admit such a shade of contempt in a question touching so near the human heart. He knows that every one is a man in the presence of sorrow and the conundrum of fate, contradiction of justice, tearing of death, and uneasiness of hope. He believes that the only way to cross the precipice is the flight with the wings of faith, the precipice made between the submission to general and absolute laws and the confidence in the infinite goodness of the Father.

The time passes and carries with it people and doctrines and systems.   Many authors left as the heritage to civilization rows of books, and in those books scepticism, indifference, doubt, lack of precision and decision.

But the last symptoms in the literature show us that the Stoicism is not sufficient for our

generation, not satisfied with Marcus Aurel-
ius's gospel, which was not sufficient even to
that brilliant Sienkiewicz's Roman *arbiter ele-
gantiarum,* the over-refined patrician Petron-
ius.   A nation which desired to live, and does
not wish either to perish in the desert or be
drowned in the mud, needs such a great help
which only religion gives.   The history is not
only *magister vitae,* but also it is the master of
conscience.

Literature has in Sienkiewicz a great poet—
epical as well as lyrical.

I shall not mourn, although I appreciate the
justified complaint about objectivity in *belles
lettres.*   But now there is no question what
poetry will be; there is the question whether
it will be, and I believe that society, being
tired with Zola's realism and its caricature, not
with the picturesqueness of Loti, but with
catalogues of painter's colors; not with the

depth of Ibsen, but the oddness of his imitators—it seems to me that society will hate the
poetry which discusses and philosophizes,
wishes to paint but does not feel, makes arche-
ology but does not give impressions, and that
people will turn to the poetry as it was in the
beginning, what is in its deepest essence, to
the flight of single words, to the interior mel-
ody, to the song—the art of sounds being the
greatest art.   I believe that if in the future
the poetry will find listeners, they will repeat
to the poets the words of Paul Verlaine, whom
by too summary judgment they count among
incomprehensible originals:

"De la musique encore et toujours."

And nobody need be afraid from a social
point of view, for Sienkiewicz's objectivity.
It is a manly lyricism as well as epic, made
deep by the knowledge of the life, sustained

by thinking, until now perhaps unconscious
of itself, the poetry of a writer who walked
many roads, studied many things, knew much
bitterness, ridiculed many triflings, and then
he perceived that a man like himself has only
one aim: above human affairs "to spin the
love, as the silkworm spins its web."

S. C. DE SOISSONS.

"The University," Cambridge, Mass.

WHERE WORLDS MEET

PROEM.

During my sojourn in California I one day set out, accompanied by Captain R., my gallant friend, to visit one of our countrymen, who lived among the solitary Santa Lucia Mountains. Failing in finding him in his home we spent five days waiting in the narrow gulch, in the sole company of an Indian servant who, in his master's absence, took care of the bees and the Angora goats. Following the custom prevailing in this country we passed the hot, sultry days mostly sleeping, while at night we assembled around a cracking wood fire, listening to the captain's stories of his many adventures and experiences, as they form themselves on the boundless prairies of America.

41

These were pleasant hours for me, in those genuine Californian, warm, quiet, star-lit nights. The great wood fire shone bright and cast its glare out upon the wild, yet beautiful and refined face of the old military pioneer, who, looking up into the clear space of the sky, allowed memory to roam among events long past, among names and scenes, some of which revived in his mind old pain. I recount here one of the tales that had exercised the greatest influence upon the life of the old captain, using the same expression, so far as I remember them, and hoping that the reader will follow me with the same hearty interest the story awakened in me that Californian summer night when I first heard it.

WHERE WORLDS MEET.

CHAPTER I.

When, in the month of September, 1849, I started for America, my first destination was the city of New Orleans, which was yet in those days to a great extent a French place, and from there up the Mississippi River, to one of those extensive sugar plantations which are so common in this part of the country, and where I soon found pleasant and remunerative employment. I was young, however, and fond of adventure, so the office work in which I was engaged did not satisfy me. The thought of being fettered to one certain place was unendurable, so I finally took my axe and went out into the woods. With a number of com-

panions I spent several years around the Louisiana lakes, among alligators, serpents, and
other wild animals. We lived from hunting
and fishing, and from time to time we flooded
down the river large quantities of wood, which
was sold with good profit in New Orleans.
Our expeditions were extended over wide
areas. We penetrated even as far as Bloody
Arkansas,—then a mere wilderness and even
now a state with but a scant population. This
life was full of fatigue and danger, in bloody
concourse with the Indians and the pirates on
the Mississippi, as they prospered in those
days in Louisiana, Arkansas and Tennessee.
Time went rapidly, and my body, while naturally strong and healthy, became more and
more hardened, better and better adapted to
life out of doors. At the same time I acquired
a most accurate, detailed knowledge of the
boundless deserts and the wilderness through

which I roamed, and would have successfully
coped with any of the red warriors in the art
of reading aright this endless book of Nature.
Thanks to this proficiency, I, shortly after the
discovery of the California gold mines had
been made, was asked to act as guide for one
of the numerous companies of gold seekers
that continually left the large Eastern cities.

I accepted this offer joyfully, for the won-
ders reported from the gold lands had long
created in me a desire of visiting the far West.
In spite of the danger besetting the road, I
could not let the offer pass on to someone else,
and so there was really no choice on my part.
At present the distance between New York
and San Francisco is traversed in eight days
by railroad, and the waste districts do not begin until west of Omaha. In those days, however, it was all different. The cities and towns
which are now closely dotting the way be-

tween New York and Chicago, were then not even in existence, and Chicago, itself, which later shot out upon the earth like a mushroom, amounted to nothing but a poor, unknown settlement of fishermen; you would not even find it marked on the map. Men, wagons and mules, and their equipment, were therefore obliged to seek a road through the wilderness, where dangerous Indian tribes, the Sioux, the Aricars, the Pawnees, the Blackfeet, etc., roamed about, and where it was difficult even for a large number of men to travel. The Indians, restless in the extreme, had absolutely no fixed habitation, but traveled around, as hunters and traders, from one end of the prairie district to the other, tracking the buffalo, the antelope and other animals.

So we were exposed to no mean danger in penetrating into the remote borderlands of the wild West. Whoever undertook such an

expedition must be prepared to sacrifice nothing less than his life, or, at least, his welfare.
The great responsibility I took upon myself
was my only source of uneasiness. But as the
expedition was determined upon, there was
for me nothing else to do than finish my
preparations. These occupied me wholly during a period of two months, for the wagons
must be ordered from Pittsburg and there
were to be gathered large amounts of victuals
and a number of good horses, mules, weapons
of different kinds, beside ammunition. In the
course of the winter all preparations were,
however, ended.

I calculated on starting our party in such a
way that we should succeed in reaching the
great prairies between the Mississippi and the
Rocky Mountains, for it was to me a well
known fact that during the summer the heat
in this part of the country is so intense that

in these shadowless regions travelers are exposed to many kinds of sickness. For this
reason, in particular, I intended not to bring
my party along the southern road, which
passes through St. Louis, but to choose the
way over Iowa, Nebraska and Northern Colorado. It was the more dangerous way, so far
as the Indians were concerned, but decidedly
the healthier.

This decision at first caused great opposition in my party, but as I remained firm and
stated that they would be obliged to choose
between adopting my plan and selecting some
one else for their guide, they consented, not
without some hesitation, and so we made our
start on the first day in spring.

For me every day's work was quite hard,
at least until the people understood my manner and gained sufficient knowledge of the
way in which safety was alone insured for

our party. My personality may have aided me some in this respect, for my adventurous excursions in the South had secured me some renown among the population in general, and the name of Big Ralph, under which I was known throughout the prairie, had become a familiar one even far away from my wonted haunts. Still, as a matter of course, the leader of an emigrant party is always running the risk of exciting the animosity of some of those whose welfare he guards, and in this respect my case was no exception.

It was my duty and privilege to select the place of our nightly camps; to superintend the progress of my caravan during the day, and to keep my eyes open to whatever passed in the camp, which often extended as far as one mile or more; to appoint watchmen and to determine in what order the travelers could be allowed to sleep in the prairie schooners.

4

Americans, as you are aware, possess an indisputable talent of organization, but their energy relaxes in proportion to the hardship they are required to undergo; even the sturdiest among them grow tired and become lacking in enthusiasm, and in that case they are not pleased to travel day by day on horseback and to serve as sentinels, moreover, during the night. Everyone, then, is glad of an opportunity to separate himself from the remainder of the party and to stretch himself in a wagon the day long. In such cases the captain of the expedition must know how to unite strict discipline with a certain pleasant comradeship, in his attitude toward the Yankees; but this is no easy matter. And so it came that during our marches and while we camped in the open land I was the commander of each individual man in the party, while during our days of rest, and when we stopped at

villages or settlements, my authority would
not avail. Then every one was his own master, and very often I found myself called upon
to break the resistance of adventurous characters. I was required to demonstrate, in numerous boxing contests, the superiority of my
Magyarian fist, and consequently my esteem
grew, so that all personal attacks upon me
ceased. But otherwise I had become so familiar with the popular American character,
and knew so well how to act in each separate
case, and besides, there was a certain pair of
blue eyes which often peeped at me through
one of the canvas wagon covers, that my power and perseverance might well obtain against
every unpleasant thing. Those eyes, which
looked out beneath a forehead framed in gold-
en locks, belonged to the person of a girl by
the name of Lilian Morris, who came from
Massachusetts. She was a fine, weakly little

thing, with clear-cut features and a sorrowful expression in her almost childish face.

This downcast demeanor in a girl so young had excited my interest already at the outset of our expedition; but my duties as guide and leader soon turned my attention to matters of a quite different character. For several weeks we scarcely exchanged other words than the obligate "good morning." But her youth and her complete isolation roused my sympathy more and more. None of the party was related to her in any way, and from time to time I lent her my assistance in various ways. Not that I found any occasion to enforce my authority as captain of the expedition, or to use my fist in protecting her against the young fellows, for in America any young woman, even if she is not subject of the urbanity that characterizes the Frenchmen, may consider herself perfectly safe in the company

of men. With due regard to Lilian's weak
looks, I gave her a place in the best, most comfortable wagon we had, and arranged with
my own hands a snug seat for her, where she
might rest at night with perfect ease. I also
allowed her the use of a buffalo skin, of which
I had several. Although these services are
hardly worth mention, Lilian appeared to receive them with great appreciation and allowed no opportunity to pass without proving
this to me. She was a very soft-hearted, reserved creature, so the two women, "Aunt
Grosvenor" and "Aunt Atkins," who shared
the wagon with her, soon became her friends
and champions and took her into their hearts,
naming her their "little bird." The latter
name was that under which she soon became
known throughout the camp. But, in spite
of it all, not the slightest approach took place
between the "little bird" and myself,—until at

length I became aware that the lustrous,
beautiful eyes of this girl rested upon me with
especial sympathy and followed me with
steady interest. This might be explained by
the fact that among all the men belonging to
our party I was the only one that commanded
some social polish. Lilian, who bore the mark
of a careful education, seemed to recognize in
me one of her equals,—the only one, in fact,
among her surroundings. Still, at that time
I explained her interest in me from quite a
different point of view. Her behavior toward
me flattered my vanity, and so I soon began
to meet the look from her beautiful eyes with
some selfish hope. In a short while I was
quite unable to account before myself for the
fact that I, having very little of sentiment
about me, could permit myself to be animated
in this manner by the girl's presence. Be it as
it might, however, I was fond of being sta-

tioned in the neighborhood of her wagon. In
the hot hours of the day—although it was
early in the year, the heat troubled us a great
deal, especially at noon, when the mules
moved but slowly, and the caravan spread
itself over a so large area that one standing at
the first wagon was hardly able to see the last
one, I would often rush from one place to
another, in order to pass Lilian and catch a
glimpse of her golden hair and the remarkable eyes, which would not efface themselves
in my remembrance. My imagination was at
first roused and moved far more than my
heart was, yet the thought that there was
among all these strangers one little heart
which sympathized with mine and interested
itself on my behalf, could not but create in
me a most pleasant anticipation. And however this hope might be viewed, it rested not
upon egoism, but sprang from the necessity

that is felt by every human being,—that of being befriended to a human being whose spirit and heart is not directed toward things general and impersonal, but concentrate themselves upon the one beloved being, and, instead of seeking their goal far away, find their own image in the heart of the chosen one.

I felt less lonely than before, and the whole expedition gained in importance to me personally.

Hitherto, when our caravan spread itself as already mentioned, and the last wagons disappeared far away, it appeared to me a lack of care and caution, and it roused my anger. Now these high, loaded wagons, with their white canvas covering, glided across the endless sea of grass like a flotilla of ships; these men, mounted on beautiful steeds, well armed, strong and sturdy, who surrounded the wagon train far and near.—all this was to me a

source of genuine pleasure. I did not realize
how these thoughts entered my head, but
often I compared myself to one of the patri-
archs who conducted the tribe that had been
entrusted to his care through the promised
land. The small bells on the yokes of our
mules, and the ever repeated call, "Get up!"
on the part of the wagoners, accompanied my
thoughts, which came from a heart that had
accustomed itself to things romantic from its
earliest days.

The presence of the other ladies prevented
me, however, from addressing Lilian in the
same language she used toward me.   And
besides, from the very moment when I realized
that there was a secret between us, I was
seized by a singular embarrassment. I doubled
my care of the ladies, looked into their wagon
as often as possible and inquired about the
health of the old ladies. in order to create a

natural reason for the care which was expend-
ed upon Lilian.   They, however, comprehended my tactics quite well, and this was
the first secret which separated us from the
rest of our companions.

Yet the looks we exchanged, the few words
which passed between us, and the care I gave
Lilian compensated for all the words that
might have been spoken. This light-haired
girl with the sweet expression in her eyes
drew me a power that could not be resisted.
The thought of her haunted me day and
night, and even late at night, when I was tired
of riding as well as of ordering my men about,
and after I had called my last "All right," in
hoarse tones, wrapped myself in my buffalo
skin and stretched myself on my couch,—even
then, when sleep and rest neared, the hum-
ming of the mosquitoes and other winged ver-
min contained to me only her sweet name. In

my dreams her figure stood near me, and my
first thought in the morning was directed toward her. And yet, how singular that I did
not realize at first what a mild, wonderful air
everything about me assumed, and the rosy
hue which rested over the very trivial objects
on my way;—the thousand new thoughts
which always drew her picture after them,
and that did not emanate from friendship or
from mere sympathy, but from that powerful
passion which no one can resist, when his turn
comes to realize it.

I might have realized my feelings before,
perhaps, if Lilian's attractive mien had not
won for her the devotion of everyone else.
Thus it appeared to me that, instead of being,
in my relations to her, on an equal footing
with the rest of the company, I was under the
influence of a special charm,—I knew not
what. From day to day I received proof of

the devotion all were ready to bestow upon
her. Her fellow travelers, the two ladies, were
persons of simple minds, neither intelligent
nor stupid, and yet I often noticed how Aunt
Atkins, this queen of she-dragons, when passing a comb through Lilian's shining hair every
morning, pressed a motherly kiss upon her
forehead, while Aunt Grosvenor would fondle
the little hand, which had become cold during
the night. Even from the men Lilian received
much attention and proof of unusual
interest.

One of the members of our party was one
Henry Simpson, a young adventurer, a native
of Kansas, really a brave boy and a skillful
hunter, but so haughty, so foolishly conceited,
that during the first month I was obliged to
knock him down repeatedly, in order to show
him that there was a fist stronger than his
own, and to prove beyond doubt that there

was at least one man who was more experienced and of greater importance than himself in our party. What a ridiculous scene, however, when Harry addressed himself to Lilian! He, whom the appearance of the President himself would not have troubled to any great extent, lost before her every particle of his independent, impudent demeanor, stood before her with his head bared, and repeated, in his extreme embarrassment, over and over again the words: "I beg your pardon, Miss Morris."—He quite made the impression of a chained dog, but one could not fail to observe that this dog was willing to obey any movement of that child's hand. At times of rest he would attempt to find a place near Lilian, and to approach her with innumerable small services. He lighted her fire and selected for her a place where the smoke would give her the least trouble, gathered moss and offered her the use of his own blankets, in order to secure for her the best comfort possible. And all this he performed with so much reserve, yet so carefully, that I should not have expected this shyness from a man of his character. It roused in me a feeling, however, quite akin to envy. But although he repeatedly excited my anger, I could in no way interfere. Henry had a right, when off duty, to employ his time in any manner he chose, and to approach Lilian as often as he liked. My service, however, was almost continuous. While on march we drew the wagons in single file, often far apart, but on entering more deserted regions we held together more closely, and when halting at noon we formed a line so firm that nowhere a man could pass between each two wagons. I can scarcely describe how much trouble and work it required before such a line, which was, of course, in-

tended for defense, according to the custom
of travelers on the prairie, could form itself
and become sufficiently compact. The mules,
which are proverbially wild and stubborn,
would either oppose the quiet position, or re-
fuse to leave the track they followed; they bit
one another, kicked about them and gave
vent to shrill cries. The wagons, if turned
aside with sudden jerks, would easily tip over,
and the raising of these movable tents was not
easy work. The braying of the mules, the
cursing of the drivers, the sounding of bells
and the barking of our dogs, made a very unpleasant noise. If finally I had succeeded in
bringing things to a satisfactory point of order, the unharnessing of the animals and their
feeding and watering became the duty of those
detailed for this service. And in the meantime
a number of the men who had formed hunting
parties came up with their spoils. Fires had

been lighted, but each fire was besieged, and even I myself would scarcely ever find time to secure a bite of food.

Even more difficult yet was the task of again setting the caravan in motion, for the harnessing of the mules was even more troublesome than their falling in line, and besides the drivers were anxious to become first in the race for the better places in the caravan. So there followed a great deal of scolding, fighting and swearing, which delayed our progress much more than was desirable. It was necessary for me to keep an eye upon all this, and during the march I must keep in front of the troop in order to survey the road and find out in the right time where we could advantageously take up our station during our next halt. Often I cursed my duties as captain of the expedition, yet the thought that on the boundless prairie I was the most im-

portant man in our party, and that the fate
of all these persons who traveled over the desert in their tented wagons depended upon my
watchfulness, expanded my heart with joy and
pride.

CHAPTER II.

One day, shortly after having crossed the Mississippi, we selected for our camping grounds a place near the Cedar River, which was surrounded by a dense brush, and where we had plenty of firewood for our use. I had accompanied the men, whose duty was to provide firewood for the camp, part of the way into the wilderness, and observed, while on my way back, that our people, taking advantage of the warm, quiet evening, had nearly all left the camp to loiter about the prairie.

It was yet quite early, for as a rule we cried halt about five o'clock in the afternoon, in order to break camp once more at early dawn.— Before long I met Miss Morris. I at once jumped from the saddle, seized the horse by its bridle and went up to her, happy with the prospect of remaining for a while alone with her. So I began conversation by asking why she, in her youth and loneliness, had braved the danger of joining this expedition, which might well exhaust the power even of the strongest men.

"I should not have permitted you to join our party," said I, "if the impression had not at first been conveyed to me that you were a daughter of Aunt Atkins. It is now too late, however, to return. But will you be able to stand it all, my dear child? You must be prepared to learn that the remainder of our journey will not be as smooth as the beginning has been."

"Sir," said she, lifting her clear, sad eyes, and looking straight into mine, "I am prepared for anything. I was obliged to go, and it would be impossible for me not to continue with the rest of us. My father lives in California. In a letter which reached me by way of Cape Horn he informs me that for several months he has been suffering from an attack of fever, in Sacramento.—My poor father! He was so accustomed to the care I delighted to give him; to my little services; to my presence. It was for my sake alone that he went to California. Who knows if I shall yet find him alive! But, in any event, I feel that when I go to join him, my duty is done."

I could make no answer to this explanation. And even if I might have raised some objection, it was now too late.

So I discussed with Lilian the circumstances surrounding her father and herself. She willingly explained everything, and I learned that Mr. Morris had held the position of judge of the supreme court, in Boston; that, owing to certain incidents, he had lost his entire fortune, and thereupon gone to California, hoping to gain once more the wealth with which he desired to surround his beloved daughter, and to secure for her once more the advantages of the best society.

While sojourning in the town of Sacramento he had been prostrated by an attack of fever, and fearing that death was near, had communicated to the daughter his last blessing. So Lilian, appropriating all means at her disposal, had resolved upon joining her father in the West. At first she intended to choose the waterway, but having made the acquaintance of Aunt Atkins two days before the starting of our party, she had altered her plans. Aunt Atkins, who was a native of Tennessee, and upon whom the exaggerated reports of my friends and admirers on my heroic deeds on the Mississippi, my adventures in Arkansas, and my great experience in wandering over the prairie, had made a great impression, had persuaded the girl to join us. The old lady had explained to Lilian that I was a safe companion to ladies and mentioned me in terms as enthusiastic as if it were not a man's duty to protect a woman on any occasion where such service might be needed. Consequently her young friend had resolved at once upon going with us.

Aunt Atkins's overcharged stories, which included even the point that I was a "knight," a man of noble descent, were evidently the point on which Lilian's admiration of me was in the main based.

"My dear Miss Morris," said I, when her story was ended, "you may rest perfectly assured that no one will dare encroach upon your rights here. Not a single moment you will cease to be an object of our protection and care. As regards your father, I wish to tell you

that California is one of the most healthy
countries on earth, and that scarcely any one
ever dies with fever in those regions. But I
can assure you that in any event you shall not
lack the protection of a strong hand, as long
as I am alive and active."

"I thank you from the bottom of my heart,
Captain," said she, as we walked on through
the camp, and my heart was beating rather
more strongly than usual.

By degrees our conversation became more
and more animated, and none of us thought
that a moment later there would be a cloud
upon the bright tone of our feeling.

"Everyone here is good and kind toward
you, Miss Morris," said I, never thinking that
from this side the cloud would descend upon
us.

"Oh, yes," she replied, "everyone is kind
to me. Aunt Atkins, Aunt Grosvenor and

also Henry Simpson. Mr. Simpson is full of attention toward me."

This reference to Henry Simpson struck me like a serpent's bite.

"Henry belongs among the mule drivers," I rejoined, dryly, "and he should remain where his duty is."

Lilian, however, following the train of her own thoughts, observed the change in my humor, and continued, as if talking to herself:

"His heart is good and true. I shall remain thankful to him during the whole of my life."

"Miss Morris," said I, excited beyond resistance, "I have no objection to your joining your fate with his. But it puzzles me why you choose me, among all, as your confidant in this matter."

To this remark she made no reply, but looked at me in astonishment, and so we con-

tinued our way amidst oppressive silence. I
did not know where to begin anew, for my
heart was too full,—too full of bitterness
against both her and myself. I was humiliated
by my jealousy toward Henry Simpson, yet
it was impossible for me to hold it in check.
My position was so foolish that I resolutely
stepped back with a brief "Good-night, Miss
Morris."

"Good-night," she said softly, and turned
away her head to conceal from me the tears
she could not keep back.

I mounted my horse and galloped toward
the brush, where a number of woodcutters
were busily working, Henry Simpson among
them. But I had not progressed very far,
when my heart was seized by a nameless sorrow, as if her tears had fallen into my very
breast. I turned back my horse and in a minute was by her side once more. Jumping

from the saddle, I stepped up to her and said:
"What gives you sorrow, Lilian?"

"Oh, Captain," she returned, "I know that
you are of noble descent. Aunt Atkins told
me it was so, but you were so kind to me, so
good —"

She tried hard to keep back her tears, but
her voice failed, and she could not complete
the sentence. The poor creature was so very
distressed over my remarks, that she regarded
them in the light of aristocratic contempt on
my part, quite contrary to my intention. It
was on my part sheer jealousy, and nothing
else, so on witnessing the pain she felt I was
quite prostrated with grief and remorse. Taking her hand in mine I said, eagerly:

"Lilian, Lilian, you have not understood
what I meant. God knows that I did not
speak to you in pride. Look at me! Besides these two hands there is nothing in the

world which I can claim as my possessions.
What importance, then, attaches to my fore-
fathers? No, the pain I felt was not that of
a false pride, but had quite a different meaning.
I intended to leave you here without an explanation, but your tears brought me back.
I swear, Lilian, that the words I uttered caused
myself more pain than they gave you.—Lilian,
you should know that to me you are not indifferent. If you were, how could your feelings toward Henry affect me as they did?
You see the pain I felt by witnessing your
grief. Forgive me, then, but with all your
heart, as I ask your forgiveness with all of
mine."

I pressed my lips against the hand that
rested in mine, and it seemed that my ear-
nestness set the girl's mind at rest. She smiled
through her tears, and even I, myself, who
had scarcely room for much romantic feeling,

or considered myself capable of much in this
line, could hardly contain myself. A singular,
tender feeling crept over me. We remained
quiet for a while, but were happy in the knowledge of each other's sentiments.

Sunset drew near, however, the weather
was beautiful, and the approaching sunset im-
parted to the prairie a variety of light effects
that was quite wonderful. The extensive area
of land on both sides of the river, the brushwood surrounding the close ranks of wagons
in our camp, the long rows of wild geese that
passed in the horizon,—all seemed shrouded
in a haze of red and gold. No wind stirred the
fine, soft tufts of grass. From a distance was
heard the muffled rush of the water, as it
rushed into a cataract somewhere beyond our
camping ground. The horses in our camp
neighed, and at intervals a dog would bark
far away.—This beautiful sunset, the virgin

soil and Lilian's presence, filled me with such
a sensation of pure joy that it seemed as if my
soul would emancipate itself and roam about
the higher spheres. I felt an almost irresisti-
ble impulse to seize Lilian's hand and once
more press it to my lips, but forbore it from
fear of approaching her.   She, however,
walked beside me, outwardly quiet, but earnest and thoughtful. She had mastered her
emotion, and soon we reached our camp, talking merrily, and in a quiet, joyous frame of
mind.

This day, so rich in emotion, was destined
to end in a most agreeable manner, as our
people had arranged a so-called picnic, an out-
door entertainment. When supper, which was
rather more sumptuous than usual, had been
disposed of, a gigantic fire was lighted, around
which a group of our young people would ar-
range a ball. Henry Simpson had unsodded

several square yards of soil, strewed it with
sand from the neighboring river, and entertained a number of interested spectators with
dancing a jig, accompanied by whistling and
the clapping of hands. Holding his arms close
to the body and standing perfectly straight,
he moved his feet, now on the heel, now on the
toe, with such amazing rapidity that the eyes
could hardly follow his step. The people who
stood around whistled, clapped their hands
and roared, until successively a second, a third
and a fourth dancer joined the group, and
the glee became unanimous. Little by little
the spectators armed themselves with tin
cans, kitchen utensils and articles belonging
to their equipment for gold-washing, or with
ox-ribs, which they held between two fingers
and struck with a sound resembling that of
castanets. Suddenly there was a cry: "Minstrel, minstrel," whereupon a ring was formed

around the dancing place. Here Jim and Crow, two negroes belonging to our party, were standing alone, one with a little drum covered with snake skin, the other with the home-made castanets already mentioned. They stood quiet for a while, looking hard at each other and turning their eyes, so that scarcely anything save the white was visible, then they began a negro song, accompanying it with a stamping of feet and a twisting of their bodies, more or less energetical according to the sentiment of the words. The long tone, "Dinah—ah—ah!" with which each verse ended, finally became a cry which had in it a somewhat brutal strain. The dancers, according to the pitch of excitement which they reached, increased the violence of their movements, until finally they knocked their heads together with such a force that European skulls, if treated in the same manner,

would have cracked like egg shells. The black
figures, hobbling about furiously in the glare
of the fire, made quite a fantastic impression.
In the wild song, in the different tones of their
instruments, the cries of the spectators mingled themselves: "Hurrah for Jim!—Go it,
Crow!"—and, occasionally, the crack of a re-
volver would follow. And finally, when the
two negroes dropped down exhausted and
panting for breath, I treated each of them
with a taste of brandy, which rapidly restored
them to their former activity and brought
them on their feet once more. Amidst all the
din and noise someone, however, called on
me for a "speech." Now the shouting and
the music ceased as by magic, and my only
course was to drop Lilian's arm, mount the
driver's seat of one of the wagons, and address the company as best I could. As I stood
there, looking down upon those many strong,

sunburnt and bearded faces,—on these men
with fire in their eyes and knives at their belts,
—on their queer caps and clothes, the scene
reminded me strangely of a theater, and I fancied myself the leader of a gang of robbers
rather than the leader of these noble, brave
men, though many of them had, perhaps, led
a life of roaming and adventure. We formed
here a little society quite separate from the rest
of the world, entirely isolated, left to our fate,
and facing much danger. Here one arm must
support the other; each one was his brother's
neighbor, and the desert surrounding us in
lonely majesty inspired into each man's breast
a feeling of mutual brotherhood with its duties. The appearance of Lilian, this young,
lonely girl, who dwelled among us as con-
fidingly as she might stay beneath her parents'
roof, contributed much to complete these sentiments, and so I spoke exactly as I felt, and

6

as it behooved a man of military rank, who
acts as a guide for his comrades and brethren.   Every little while I was interrupted by
such cries as, "Hurrah for the Polander! Hurrah for the Captain! Hurrah for Big Ralph!"—
What inspired my words more than anything
else was, however, the sight of a pair of small
white hands among the many large brown
ones.   It was clear to me, as never before,
whence I should receive the courage and
strength that was necessary in making us pass
unmolested through the desert and the wilderness, with their inhabitants of wild beasts and
Indians, scarcely less wild, and the "outlaws,"
who recognized no one's rights.   In genuine
enthusiasm, I cried to the listeners that I felt
strong enough to brave every danger; that I
would crush whatever obstructed our progress, and that I would lead the expedition
safely to its destination, were it even at the

world's end. I presented myself ready to receive God's punishment, if I did not state the
truth. Yet more enthusiasm and cries of hurrah were called forth by this address. Amidst
general exhilaration we intonated the emigrant's song,

> I crossed the Mississippi,
> I shall cross Missouri—;

whereupon Smith, the oldest man in our party,
a miner from the Pittsburg region, jumped up
and thanked me in the name of our expedition,
spoke of my ability as a leader and proposed
a general cheer. When Smith had finished,
nearly everyone climbed into a wagon, prepared to deliver an oration of some kind, such
as his feelings prompted. Some made hum-
orous speeches, especially Henry Simpson,
who continually seconded himself by this
strong assertion:

"Gentlemen, I will be hanged, if this is not the truth!"

At length, the speakers became hoarse, the music began anew, with the dancing. The night had come, and the moon shone so bright that even our large fire looked pale when compared to it. The effect of the silver light, on one side, and the red glare, on the other, was quite singular.

The night was one of rare beauty. The mad merriment in our camp formed a queer, but in no respect a disagreeable, contrast to the deep quiet of the prairie. I took Lilian's arm, and we walked the whole circuit around the camp, glancing from the fire into the dark shadows beneath the tall, wavy grass on which the moonlight shed its silverspun rays, imparting to it a fantastic, unreal air. As they walked along, two Scotsmen, Highlanders, began to sing their singular lay, "Bon Dundee," full of longing and softness, accompanying themselves on their lutes. We stood quite still, listening to their song, when of a sudden I caught her glance with mine. She looked down, and hardly knowing how I grasped her hand, which rested on my arm, dropped it and folded the girl in my embrace. I felt the throbbing of Lilian's heart; stronger and stronger it grew, and we both trembled, feeling that a great change passed within us, and that we would never again face each other as strangers. I already swam in the new element, with all sails set, into which the flood had carried me. I forgot how near was the camp, how light the night, how bright the fire, but held her close to me and looked eagerly into her eyes. She made no resistance, but turned her face aside, into the shade, as if anxious that no one should see her. I struggled for words, but could not find words worthy of my feelings. It seemed as if a voice, strange to me, would utter the words, "I love you,"—but that the power of speech was denied me. I was young, and, in matters of the heart, quite reserved. It was clear to me, however, that if the words, "I love you," had once been spoken, my past life would disappear behind a thick veil, while my future would lie open behind the great, golden gates Lilian and I would enter together,—a new province of my existence, unknown and unexplored. But, although beckoned onward by happiness, I stopped. The very brightness of the prospect blinded my sight. Besides, if the longing for love is to find its way, not over the lips, but upward from the heart, its expression in words becomes more difficult than ever.

I had dared to take the girl in my arms, and yet we both were silent, as I had not yet dared to say what my thoughts dwelled upon, and there was nothing else for us to speak of.

And so we remained together one brief while, until someone in the camp called my name. The festivities were nearly over.

To end the evening's pleasure in a fitting manner the men wanted to sing a few hymns. So the men bared their heads, and, although the most different confessions were represented among us, we all kneeled together on the prairie soil and joined in the psalm, "Walking through the desert."

It was a touching scene. When the pauses came, everything was so quiet that we could hear the sputtering of the sparks in the fire and the distant roar of the cataracts.

Kneeling by Lilian's side, I looked at her from time to time. Her eyes shone with a soft, wonderful glow; the hair was a little out of order, and while singing with the rest of us she looked a true picture of an angel.

When the hymn ended, our people retired
to the wagons. As customary I made a round
in the camp, whereupon I lay down to rest.
And, while thinking of Lilian that night, I
realized that in the wagon near by slept my
greatest treasure on earth, the soul of my soul,
—and that to me there was no more beloved
being in the whole wide world than this only
woman.

CHAPTER III.

On the following day, by sunrise, we crossed the Cedar River and entered the extensive prairie regions which lay between this and the central valleys, with some deviation toward the south, where they border upon the forest regions extending through the southern part of Iowa.

Lilian scarcely dared to meet my glance. I observed that she was thoughtful; that she felt hurt or ashamed, I knew not what. And yet, God knew we had committed no sin.— She scarcely at all left the wagon, and the two "aunts," who feared she might be suffering, gave her the most careful attention. But no one except myself knew what her condition meant; that she suffered neither bodily pain, nor was pained by a bad conscience, but merely struggled, in her purity, against the new power that had entered her life, threatening to tear her away from herself.

It was to this girl something of a revelation that sooner or later the hour would strike when, forgetting everything else, she would yield to this power, and permit it to rule her every action.

Every pure soul is frightened when realizing that new feelings enter into its existence. It is frightened at the thought of being unable to withstand this power. So Lilian was like one dreaming, while I, on my part, would almost hold my breath in meditating on what happiness had fallen to my share. It was a queer sensation, yet God knows I struggled to disregard it, that whenever passing Lilian's wagon I saw myself in the light of a bird of prey, which is sure of its dove. She sat there, like a broken flower.—Yet I could not have roughly touched a feather of that dove of mine for all the treasures of the world. My love was mingled with a feeling of intense pity for this helpless, confiding being. Singularly enough, this whole day passed, as if we had hurt each other's feelings, in spite of the fact that I gave to her my tenderest thoughts. It seemed that we could not find each other, as we had done the night before. I pondered and pondered how all this could be, and devised one plan after another, that would enable me to be alone with Lilian even for the briefest possible moment; but nothing would avail. Happily, Aunt Atkins came to my assistance, declaring that the closeness of the wagon would make the little one sick, and that she must be given an opportunity to move about. I eagerly seized the opportunity of having a horse

saddled for Lilian. A Mexican saddle with a
high pommel, such as was commonly used by
women in this part of the country, was made
available, as we did not command the use of
a lady's riding outfit. So the difficulty was
overcome, and I asked Lilian to remain as
close to me as possible, in order that I might
always ascertain her safety.

The danger of losing one's way in the
prairie was, however, not very great, for those
detailed by me to form hunting parties surrounded our caravan on all sides, and although
the country was perfectly devoid of tracks or
roads, and consequently it would be quite dangerous to become isolated from one's companions, our people would always be sure to
meet one or another of our smaller parties.

Even from the Indians we needed not to
fear anything, as the part of the country surrounding us was visited by the Pawnees only

during the hunting season. They were yet
abundantly supplied with game in their re-
sorts near the forests, and had no occasion to
cross our way.—I secretly hoped that Lilian
would follow me closely, and that I should
thus have an opportunity of speaking to her.

As a rule I rode quite far ahead of our caravan and was preceded only by the Mestizos
as pathfinders. Imagine my joy when in a little while I saw that my fair little amazon approached from far away in a light gallop. Her
hair had become loosened by her ride, and the
light dress was floating in the wind, which
occasioned a beautiful expression of embarrassment in her eager, smiling face. Approaching nearer, she blushed like a rose,
knowing well enough that I had led her into a
trap and desired to be alone with her, and half
glad, half resentful, she came up to me,—did
not hesitate. but came nearer and nearer, in

spite of herself. My own heart, however, beat
violently, and when finally our horses stood
side by side I knew not what to say, but was
angry, vexed with myself. But the feeling
that held both of us in sway was too strong,
so I bent forward, under the pretense of
tightening a clasp about her saddle, but really
for the purpose of pressing my lips on her
hand. My heart expanded with an overmas-
tering thrill of joy. I continued to hold her
hand and said to her, even if God held all the
treasures of this earth in store for me, I would
not relinquish her for their sake, for she belonged to me, body and soul, forever.

"Lilian," said I, "I am prepared to follow
you over land and sea; to walk in your foot-
steps and devote my whole life to your welfare.
Only say that you love me, or that, at least, I
am not wholly indifferent to you."

I scarcely knew how I gathered courage

enough to utter these words, but Lilian said softly, without daring to meet my glance:

"Oh, Ralph, you know it quite well; you know it all."

I hardly could persuade myself of what to do. Should I gallop away, out over the prairie, or remain where I was, or what? As I hope to-day for eternal peace, I vow that in that moment I could imagine no greater blessing or joy than was already mine.

Since that day we remained together as often as my duties would permit. And my duties grew less and less burdensome, as we neared the Missouri River. Hardly ever did an expedition through the prairie region succeed as well as ours, so far as we had come. Men and animals alike seemed to obey orders willingly and readily, and became so well accustomed to our mode of traveling, that there would be no further need of looking after

them. The good spirit manifesting itself in all
my relations to the party that had entrusted
itself to my care was a source of pleasant feeling on all sides. The beautiful weather that
accompanied us all the time, and our abundant supply of food supported our health and
our good humor alike. I was convinced that
my plan of bringing our caravan to its destination, by way of the northern road, instead
of the southern, which went through the city
of St. Louis, had proved itself an excellent
one. Iowa and Nebraska were healthy states,
quite different from the South, where the sun
burned hotly, and the warm region between
the Mississippi and Missouri rivers threatened
with fever and many other dangerous
scourges. In the North the cooler climate had
a most beneficial effect upon the health and
lessened the strain of the long, varying
marches.

It must be conceded that the way leading through St. Louis was less threatened by attacks from the Indians; but our party numbered some three hundred strong, well armed men, and besides the Indians who lived in Iowa were so well accustomed to the sight of white men and the power of their fists, that they dared not rush against a larger number of travelers. There was a greater danger, however, of nightly attacks intended for the abduction of our mules and horses, and in this respect the greatest care was necessary, as nothing is worse to a body of prairie travelers than the loss of their draught animals. Against such calamity we were, however, amply guarded by the vigilance of our sentinels, the majority of whom were familiar with the cunning and the tricks of the Indians.

Now, the details of our organization having been settled once for all, and the people hav-

7

ing become familiar with their various duties,
I had less to do than before, and could devote
more time to analyze the sentiment that so
completely had mastered me. Thinking, "To-
morrow you will see Lilian," I lay down to rest,
and in the morning I awoke with a longing for
her; every day I was deeper and deeper in
love. In the course of time our relations were
known in the camp, among our fellow travelers, but no one grudged against what had
happened, for Lilian and I were equally well
liked among the people. One day old Smith,
in passing by, cried to us: "God bless you,
Captain, and your Lilian!" and this association
of our names made us happy all the rest of the
day. The old aunts would often whisper
something to Lilian, which made her blush,
but never would she repeat what they had
said. Henry Simpson only looked downcast
and would from time to time glance at us un-

easily; perhaps something weighed upon his mind, but I did not think of investigating into it.

At four o'clock every morning I put our caravan in motion. A thousand feet in advance of me were the two pathfinders, and behind me the train of wagons and riders forming a light band along the prairie. The pathfinders sang continually,—old lays which they had learned from their mothers. And how wonderful it was when about six o'clock I heard a light clatter of hoofs and knew that the joy of my heart and of my eyes was coming,—my own, beloved girl, whose smiles were a fountain of delight to me. Her hair was streaming down over her shoulders, and of course the wind was blamed for the mischief, but I knew that the little innocent one had on purpose arranged it carelessly, knowing that I liked to see it in this manner. I affected not to see her, and with this sweet roguery the day began. I had taught her to say "Dzien dobry"* in Polish, and when this well known greeting reached my ear, she who uttered it was dearer to me than ever. I awakened the memory of my old home, of my relatives there, of times past, and often I was on the point of bursting into tears, only I was ashamed of this weakness, and when Lilian observed that, although I was deeply moved, joy was still uppermost in my heart, she repeated the words over and over again, like a bird which has learned talking. And why should I not love my little bird from the very depth of my heart? As time passed I taught her yet a number of words and phrases, and when her American tongue refused to give utterance to the difficult sounds of my native language, and I had occasion to laugh at her

*Good morning.

comical pronunciation, she would, in her sweet
way, affect to be angry, while really we were
never impatient with each other. Only once a
cloud ascended upon the bright sky of our
happiness, namely, when one morning she
joined me, as usual, in front of the caravan,
and one of the straps on her one stirrup was
loosened. I jumped off to set matters right,
but instead of attending to the stirrup I bent
down and kissed the little foot which had
made so many weary marches across the desert. But she tore her foot away.

"No, Ralph, no, no!" she cried.

Then, turning her horse around, she flew
back to her wagon, and, in spite of my repeated calling, would not return. In spite of
my assurance that I meant no harm, she galloped out of sight and refused to return to
me. But in order not to cause me a too great
humiliation she did not enter her wagon. Rid-

ing apart, with her head bent, she never stirred
to approach me, and I, seemingly remorseful,
attended to my duties with the air of a man
who had lost every chance in the world. I
need hardly say that my remorse was not
quite genuine, and that I was convinced she
would soon return to me. And so it happened. Quite alarmed over my passive bearing, she came slowly down to me, nearer and
nearer, like a child that wishes to make sure if
its mother is yet angry and desires to "make
up."—She tried to catch a glimpse of my eyes,
and, though preserving my earnest demeanor,
I must exercise the very greatest self-control
in order to avoid bursting into a fit of merriment.—But such episodes happened only
once. As a rule, we were happy and contented
in each other's company, and in many instances I, the captain of an expedition crossing the American continent, behaved like a

child in the girl's company. Often, as we rode
along without thinking of anything special, I
would turn toward her saying that I had something very important to communicate. Then,
as she faced me in the expectation of receiving some important information, I would say
to her, in a subdued tone: "I love you." And
she would answer, blushing with pride and
joy: "I love you, too!"

Such were the secrets we shared with each
and with the lonely prairie and with the wind
that waved the tall, soft grass.

With a swiftness incredible to me, morning,
evening, days and weeks passed, touching
each other like electric sparks. Rarely did
anything disturb our pleasant, uniform con-
cord. One Sunday, Wickit, one of the Mestizoes, had caught with his lasso a large antelope, commonly named "Dick" in the prairie,
and her young ones. I gave the animal to

Lilian, who made for her a collar with a bell
taken from the harness of one of the mules,
and called her Kitty. In the course of a week
the antelope became quite tame, so tame, in
fact, that she ate out of our hands. During
our marches she, with her young ones, kept
near Lilian and watched her mistress with her
large black eyes.

The uniformity of the landscape continued,
only that the warm summer, which was close
upon us, made the grass run up to its full
height. Our pathfinders would occasionally
disappear amidst the vegetation, which waved
before the wind like an ocean. I explained to
Lilian such secrets as I knew of this unknown
world, which in its every feature was new to
her, and when she expressed her admiration
of it all, I was proud that my kingdom pleased
her so well. Spring had passed, and the greatest wealth the prairie could afford lay before

us to all sides,—a world of singular, wild
beauty.

The fragrance of the flowers toward night-
fall was almost overwhelming, and on such
days, when the wind blew across this ocean
of stalk and foliage, one was impressed with
the richness of the soil we traversed. From
the ground rose tall, elastic stalks crowned
with clusters of yellow flowers. Around
them a plant called "tears" twined itself, with
flowers in the shape of small, diaphanous
flowers that really looked like tear drops.
My eyes, which had long since accustomed
themselves to the prairie, was met every little
while by new, unknown flowers and herbs,
here the large leaves so useful in healing
wounds, there white and red little flowers
famous for other virtues, and again the "Indian Axe," the fragrance of which almost be-
numbs the senses. Here I taught Lilian to

read Nature's open book,—God's great nature.

"As you will in time come to live in the
woods and on the prairie, my dear," said I to
her, "it is not too early to become familiar
with some of their peculiarities."

Here and there groups of trees would rise
out of the many-colored bottom vegetation,
their trunks and branches overgrown with
wild wine and other vines, ivy and the stately
climber Wachtia, which resembles the wild
rose. In among these trees was dim like in a
church; outside the flowers hung down in
great abundance. Around the trees were
large pools of water that the sun had not yet
been able to dry out, and from the tree-tops
and in among the foliage the most singular
tones were heard, a twittering and warbling,
a chanting and chirping from the numerous
birds that made their homes amidst this

wealth of vegetation. The first time Lilian, in my company, saw such a group of trees with their cascade of flowers and foliage intertwined, she clapped her hands and exclaimed:

"Oh, Ralph, can this be possible?"

She was afraid, however, to go in among the trees, but one day at noon, when the sun was very hot and a glowing hot Texas-wind blew from the South, we both went in among the shadows, closely followed by Kitty.

We stopped at the edge of a pond which reflected our images. Both of us were on horseback. Under the trees it was as cool and solemn as in a Gothic church, and the surroundings, clothed in the dusk, assumed an uncanny air. Daylight penetrated but sparingly into the arbor; above us hung the foliage in a dense, greenish mass, and from time to time the chirp of a bird would be heard from outside the rustling dome, like a cry of

warning. Kitty trembled all over her body;
but Lilian's eyes met mine, and for the first
time she allowed my lips to touch hers. Our
souls, as it were, soared heavenward, clinging
to each other, never to part again. My dear
girl's eyes were veiled with tears, her hands,
which folded themselves around my neck,
trembled like in a fever, and she leaned her
head upon my shoulder, as if she had at last
found the support she needed in her loneliness. We both were lost in the feeling of our
mutual happiness. I scarcely dared to move;
my whole being was so saturated with a feeling of supreme joy that it seemed natural
for me to thank God for the great, pure
love He had inspired into my poor, mortal
heart.

In a little while we left the trees and rode
out into the open land, where a new light and
a fresh breeze surrounded us once more. The

view was a beautiful one. In all directions the
same refreshing view of the blooming prairie,
—and behind us the twitter of legions of
happy birds.

At a distance we observed a number of
small promontories, with small openings into
the ground. About these stood in long rows,
with almost a military bearing, large numbers
of ground squirrels, which disappeared within
their abodes when we drew nearer. And far
away came the train of our expedition, flanked
by expert riders.

I felt as if we had suddenly emerged from
a dark enclosure out into the world's beautiful
light, and Lilian's thoughts went in the same
direction. But upon me the daylight had an
exhilarating influence, while Lilian, facing the
sunlight and thinking of our passionate meeting, bowed her head in fear and embarrassment.

"Ralph," she suddenly said, "how badly I behave. What must you think of me?"

"How can you think so, my sweet friend!" said I. "May God forget me if I have anything but good and kind thoughts in my heart,—if I entertain any other feeling but love and reverence for you."

"It only happened," pleaded she, "because I love you so much." Her lips trembled, and she wept softly. And in spite of all I did to set her mind at rest, she remained downcast and thoughtful during the remainder of the day.

CHAPTER IV.

At length we reached the Missouri. As a
rule the Indians choose for their attacks the
time when caravans are about to cross the
river, because at such time the defense is more
lax than at any other time. When some of
the wagons have reached the opposite side,
and another detachment is yet in the stream;
when the animals become excited, and require
the undivided attention of the drivers and the
other attendants alike, the means of defense
are usually so much diminished that an attack may be successfully made. Having noticed that during the last days of our march
our track was continually followed by swarms
of Indians, I took every precaution and intro-
duced among our men a perfectly military or-

der. I forbade the straying about of the wagons outside the limits of our expedition and told the men that we had reached a dangerous part of the country, where every one must be continually prepared for a fight. When we came into view of the river, and a safe fording place had been found, I ordered a detachment of sixty men to take up their position at each side of the stream and to throw up ramparts with a sufficient number of embrasures to make our further movements perfectly well protected. A party of one hundred and ten was to take our property, wagons, animals, etc., across the water. A few wagons only were taken over at one time, in order to avoid any kind of confusion. Under such precautions as these everything passed in perfect order, and the possibility of either side being successfully attacked was at once precluded. Either of our small fortresses must necessarily suffer a siege or an attack, before any routing of our forces could be accomplished. To what extent all this caution was necessary became known to the masses two years later, when a party of four hundred German settlers was completely annihilated during their attempt of fording the river. This happened on the very spot where the city of Omaha was afterward built. We, however, were so much better protected, because people from the East, who had heard much of the great danger involved in crossing the yellow waters of the Missouri, were, on account of the promptness and great facility with which we overcame all obstacles, convinced of my ability in precluding every possible danger. In fact, their trust in me was almost unlimited, and in some instances a murmur reached my ear to the effect that I had at my command the service of a higher power.

8

Lilian received constant expressions of the high regard in which I was held by my men. Her loving eyes viewed me in a hero's capacity. One day Aunt Atkins said to her:

"As long as your Pole is near, you may sleep safely without fear of rain and wind. He will see to it that nothing harms you." My girl's heart expanded with joy and pride when such tributes of praise were offered to me. During the whole time of the fording I was unable to give any attention to her; only from time to time I gave her a glance expressing what the lips were prevented from uttering. I spent the whole day on horseback, now in the water, now on this, now on the other side of the river. I was anxious that we should leave the yellow, muddy stream as soon as possible, for the large masses of rottening wood, foliage, mud and dirt made the place a veritable hotbed of fever miasms.

Yet the people became quite exhausted
with the uninterrupted activity; the horses,
unaccustomed to this kind of exercise, were
sick and grew worse in consequence of drink-
ing the river water, which we ourselves could
not use except after it had been thoroughly
boiled.

At length, after eight days' incessant activity, we had successfully overcome all obstacles
and pitched our camp on the opposite shore.
Our only cause of regret was a few broken
wagons and the loss of seven mules. But on
the very day when we completed our transfer,
the first shots were fired, and my people shot
and killed, and even scalped, three Indians,
who had sneaked into the place where our
mules were kept. I resented their cruelty
most thoroughly, but knew it would be useless
to prevent the men from adopting the fighting
methods of the savages. In consequence,

however, of what had happened, there arrived
toward evening a delegation numbering three
of the oldest and most shrewd members of
the Pawnee tribe. Taking a seat by our camp
fire with perfect ease and amidst a silence
promising of anything unpleasant, they demanded a tribute of mules and horses, to com-
pensate for the loss they had sustained; otherwise their entire force of five hundred warriors
would enforce their demand in the manner
they would deem the most expedient. The
quotation of the five hundred made, however,
no impression upon me, as our camp was well
guarded. I knew quite well that the red men
had sent out the delegation only for the purpose of attaining something without being
obliged to employ manual force, as they could
not fail to see how well we were in every respect guarded against an attack from their
side. In fact, I should have sent them away

without further preliminaries, had I not desired that Lilian should witness our counsel-
ling. Hidden in the back end of the wagon
she watched the immovable bodies sitting by
the fire and staring continuously into the
flames. Their blankets were held together by
small bands wound of human hair, the handles
of their tomahawks ornamented with many-
colored decorations, and they had painted
their faces in a manner suggestive of enmity.
In spite of these suggestions I declined, however, to grant their demands, and, passing
from a defensive to the offensive attitude I
declared most emphatically that in case a single mule were removed from our camp I should
be certain of seeking separation by appear-
ing in their midst and scattering the bones of
their five hundred warriors over the prairie.
Finally they went, suppressing with difficulty
their rage, and flourishing their tomahawks

in a manner suggestive of their warlike tendencies. The warning to which I had given
utterance was remembered by them, however,
as two hundred of our men stationed themselves at the entrance of the camp and engaged in divers threatening altercations as the
delegation left us. We uttered some wild
shouts and rattled our weapons in such a manner that our enemies could not but receive a
strong impression of our power and ability to
fight.

Several hours afterward, however, Henry
Simpson, who had gone after the Indians and
watched their movements, rushed into the
camp in breathless excitement, reporting that
a large number of Indian warriors bore down
upon us with all signs of great ardor. In the
whole camp I was the only man who had become familiar with the ways and habits of the
savages. I knew well enough that their move-

ments were indicative more of empty threats
than of actual warfare. Indians, namely, are
scarcely ever sufficiently numerous to withstand, with their bows and arrows, the white
men's means of defense. I reassured Lilian,
who trembled for my life, and told her that
although some actual fighting might occur,
since our young people had allowed themselves to be possessed by quite a warlike spirit,
and longed for an earnest fight, there was no
danger that anything serious might befall us.
In a short while we heard the war-whoops of
the redskins, but they were as yet too far away
to be reached by our firearms, and seemed
to await an opportune moment to attack us.
During the night we kept up in our camp a
gigantic fire, which was fed with driftwood
from the borders of the stream and with whatever wood we could find in the surrounding
country. The men kept guard around the

wagons. The women, who could not help being frightened, in spite of our protestations,
would pray for our safety from time to time.
As we had not allowed the mules to roam
free during the night, but kept them in an
enclosure, they kept up a perpetual concert,
stamping their feet, crying in loud tones and
fighting one another. The dogs, which
smelled the nearness of the redskins, barked
continually. Full of weird noise, as our camp
was, the night was in all respects unpleasant;
from far away came the war cries of the Indian sentinels, which promised nothing good.
Toward midnight the Indians made an attempt to set the prairie afire; but the fresh
grass refused to burn, although for several
days past we had had no rain.

Making my usual round in the early morning I found an opportunity to say a few words
to Lilian. The poor child had gone to sleep

from exhaustion. Her head rested in the lap
of old Aunt Atkins, who had armed herself
with every available weapon and swore, rather
to shoot, or knock down, the whole Indian
tribe, than permit any of the savages to touch
a hair on the little one's head. I, too, looked
at the girl's face, beautiful in its rest, not only
as the man would who loved the fair creature,
but almost with a father's tenderness, and felt,
like Aunt Atkins, ready to rise up against
those who might have desired to approach
my sweetheart. She was the source of my joy,
my hope, my strength; she was the sunshine
of my life and existence; without her my existence would have been an empty roaming
about, without goal or purpose, a play of nature and myself. How clearly did I not see
the opposing forces that struggled within and
about me! Here the endless prairie, the clatter of weapons, a night passed on horseback,

awaiting a fight with the wild Indians. And
here this lovely child of mankind resting
peacefully amidst it all, so firm in her faith in
me, so confiding that a word of mine was sufficient to dispel from her mind every doubt,
every fear of the enemy's attack, resting as
untroubled as in her parents' home.

Reflecting upon these things I felt more
clearly than ever how tired I was of this life
of adventure, and how I would regain all my
former equanimity in Lilian's company. When
we had reached California, the promised land,
everything should be different. There I should
find, with my bride, a beautiful climate, an
everlasting springtime, a mild, uniform climate. But as yet the troubles of the journey
were yet before us. We had the lighter part
of the task behind us, and yet it had left its
trace on the cheeks of her, the most important
of my many charges.

I spread a cloak over the sleeper, in order
to prevent her from coming into contact with
the night's cool breeze and returned to my
station. From the river rose a fog so dense
that the Indians might employ it as a means
of approaching us unobserved. The fire,
though burning bright, soon was seen as an
indistinct glow, and grew more and more pale.
In a short while a human body was not dis-
tinguishable at a distance even of ten feet. I
ordered the guards to call to one another continually, and soon there was no sound in the
camp than the often repeated "All's well!"
which went from one to the other like the an-
swers in the church. But among the redskins
quiet reigned so completely that I began to
feel quite uneasy. Toward daybreak we became tired and worn out with exhaustion.
Our people had suffered much loss of sleep
during the previous nights and could stand

the strain no longer. And the fog brought
with it a singular cold, which benumbed every
sense.

I reflected whether it would not be best for
us to effect a sally against the Indians, instead
of remaining quietly where we were. It would
be better to scatter their forces at once, instead
of awaiting their arrival in anxious suspense.
This was no manifestation of a taste for adventure on my part, but a real necessity, as a
successful charge from our side would imbue
the tribes far and near with a superior idea of
our military tactics, and insure us against further attack. So I selected a hundred and thir-
ty men headed by Smith, the old prairie wolf,
placed the camp under their supervision,
placed myself at the head of a select force of
one hundred and started out, eagerly and with
every nerve strained in the intense cold, in
pursuit of the redskins. At some distance

from their camping grounds we put our
horses to a furious gallop and made for them
with as much noise and shooting as could be
produced. The bullet fired by an untrained
member of our band whistled by me, but did
no damage further than to tear off my cap. A
moment later we were down upon the unsus-
pecting savages, who were altogether unpre-
pared for an attack by us. For all that I know
it might have been the first time an expedition
of our kind charged on its own accord. They
were so frightened, however, that instead of
defending themselves they ran about shriek-
ing and yelling. Only one small detachment,
which was driven back to the river and saw no
way of escaping, defended itself valiantly and
preferred to plunge into the river to asking
our pardon. Their light lances and their small
stone axes were not very dangerous weapons,
but they used them with wonderful skill. Yet

in less time than it takes to tell it, we had
routed them completely, and I even succeeded
in capturing one of their number, who suffered, in a hand-to-hand fight, the loss of his
tomahawk as well as of the hand that held it.
We captured a number of horses, but they
were so wild that no use could be made of
them. We made twenty prisoners all in all,
every one of whom was more or less danger-
ously wounded. We gave them the most careful attention and provided them, in view of
their condition, with blankets and horses,
whereupon they were at liberty to go whither
they pleased. The poor devils, who were prepared for a painful death, and had already begun to chant their melancholy death-songs,
were at first quite frightened at our behavior
toward them. They thought that we only set
them free in order to hunt them down afterward, according to Indian custom, but realiz-

ing that no danger was threatening they departed with many words in praise of our val-
iant fighting and of the beauty of the "white
flower." namely, Lilian, who had interceded in
their behalf.

This day was destined, however, to end in a
manner throwing a great shadow over our joy
of the victory we had won and its hoped-for
results. In our troop none had been killed,
but a number were wounded, and among
these Henry Simpson, whose habitual passion
had led him to forget all necessary patience.
Toward evening his condition became so
hopeless that he was perfectly prostrated. He
seemed desirous of being confessed, but was
scarcely able to utter a word clearly. His
skull had been fractured by the blow from a
tomahawk. Hardly had he uttered the words,
"Pardon me, Captain——," that brought me
to his side, when his limbs were seized by

cramps and he was unable to continue. I
thought of the bullet that had passed close by
my head on the previous morning, but par-
doned this with all my heart. For I knew
that with him would be buried the love he felt,
which centered itself upon Lilian and was not
to be uttered in this world. Perhaps he had
sought death with a fixed purpose. He died
at midnight, and we buried him under a large
tree, into the bark of which I carved a cross.

CHAPTER V.

On the following day we broke camp, and before us lay the prairie once more, vaster, greater, more imposing, however, than before, a boundless and wayless extension of virgin soil, as scarcely was to be found anywhere else on earth. At first we proceeded quite rapidly across the woodless plains, but not without some difficulty, inasmuch as there was a constant lack of firewood. The banks of the Platte River, which traverses the entire stretch of this region, was surrounded by rush and scant brushwood, but as this river had transgressed its natural boundaries, as usually during springtime, we were obliged to keep away from the water's bed. We fed our fires with whatever available material we

9

could find. Amidst the greatest difficulties we
reached the so-called Big Blue River, where,
it was hoped, we should succeed in finding
ample stores of fuel. The land through which
we passed seemed to be altogether untouched
by civilization. From time to time large herds
of antelopes passed in the immediate neighborhood of our party; here and there the
huge, bulky, shaggy head of a buffalo arose
above the grass with bloodshot eyes and
damping nostrils. And again, long rows or
immense herds of these animals would be seen
dotting the prairie far away.

From time to time we would pass by extensive cities of prairie dogs' abodes. The Indians kept themselves entirely out of view,
and one day, when three red riders in gor-
geous feather and skin attire came down upon
us seemingly unawares, they made off with
the speed of lightning. In the course of our

journey westward I subsequently learned that
the bloody lesson we had taught them on the
banks of the Missouri had made the name of
"Big-ar," which was their pronunciation of
my name, feared among them, while, on
the other hand, our gentle treatment of
the prisoners had aroused the kindness
of the ungoverned, yet in some respects
considerate and withal quite romantic redskins.

After having reached the woody banks of
the Big Blue River we made a ten days' stop.
The last part of the way, which lay before us,
was a more difficult one, for behind the prairie
arose the Rocky Mountains and the "bad
lands" of Utah and Nevada. Our mules and
horses had suffered greatly in spite of their
abundance of feed; they were exhausted,
emaciated, and had great need of both rest and
invigoration. So we pitched our camp in a

triangle formed between the two rivers, Big
Blue and Beaver Creek. This excellent position shielded from two sides by the streams,
from the third by a compact wall of wagons,
seemed all the more impregnable, because
wood and fuel were present in abundance. We
pretended no great activity, as there was no
need of any kind of work, so the members of
the expedition enjoyed life and liberty according to their individual tastes. These, indeed, were the happiest days of our whole
journey. The weather remained well, and the
nights became warm enough to permit our
sleeping under the open sky.

In the morning such of us as desired to
wield the gun would go out hunting and return home laden with spoils of antelopes
and birds in great variety; they would then
spend the afternoon eating, singing or doz-
ing under the trees, or amusing themselves

with shooting at the wild geese that passed
us in large numbers.

I cannot recall a period in my whole existence so happy as this. From early till late I
remained not for a single moment away from
Lilian, and this beginning of our life in common, which was indeed more than a passing
vision of happiness, convinced me that I had
indeed succeeded in winning the full affection
of this tender, precious being. Better and better I learned to see the rare qualities of her
inner life. Again and again I awoke in my
sleep meditating how indeed I had deserved
such affection, and what qualities of mine
would make me so dear to her;—how it was
that I could, indeed, be as indispensable to
her as the air she breathed. God knows that
I loved to see her beautiful face, her splendid
long tresses of hair and her sparkling eyes;
her slender, swaying form,—her whole being,

which seemed to appeal to me for support, as she could not live without me. God knows that I revered herself, her manner, her speech and sentiment; that it all drew me so irresistibly that I hardly realized anything else. And yet I think that her meekness, more than anything else, held me in sway, the softness of her manner toward all, and the great tenderness of her feeling. I have met many women in my lifetime, but never a tender, soft-hearted girl like this,—and I now think of it with a nameless pain in my heart, that I shall never meet the like of her. Her soul was pure and sensitive, her life and thoughts stainless; her very presence an education in itself.

Every thought, every word of mine produced a reverberation in her heart, an image, but clearer and truer than the original. And she yielded to the passion of her soul with so much virtuous resistance that I felt her

love must really be great in order to conquer
her woman's instinct of purity and sacrifice it
for the higher purpose, that of becoming one
with me. In such relations all that a man possesses of honor and reverence dissolves into a
boundless thankfulness to her whom he has
chosen. My Lilian remained so tender and
loving, so reserved and careful of herself, that
I must always assure her that our love was no
sin, and always took care to tell her this in
such a manner as would not create in her the
thought that I was trifling with the bond that
held us together. And so the ten days we
passed together on the banks of the two rivers
passed in such a manner that I cannot forget
them until my dying hour.

One day, as the sun was rising, we walked
along Beaver Creek, where Lilian wanted to
show me a beaver settlement which was erected about half-a-mile from our camping

grounds. Passing cautiously along the edge of the creek we reached our destination in a little while. At this place the river, in flooding some low ground, formed a diminutive lake surrounded by gigantic sycamores. The edge of this lake was covered with willows overhanging the water. The beaver house had been built up against the upper course of the creek, and above it was made an artificial dam, which served for the purpose of keeping the water at an even height, so that the abode itself, with its little cupola, as provided by these skillful, diligent animals, would always remain as far below the surface as was desirable.

In all probability no human foot had ever before touched this secluded spot, overgrown with the vegetation of centuries. Cautiously bending away the branches before us we looked out upon the smooth, sparkling

stream. The beavers had not yet begun work;
the little society in the water was yet at rest,
and a perfect quiet reigned all around,—a
quiet so complete that we could hear each
other breathing. Lilian thrust her head forward through the dense foliage and leaned on
me. Her head touched mine lightly. I put
my arm around her slender form to prevent
her from losing her foothold on the slippery
bank, and so we waited patiently, watching
Nature's revelations about us. Being accustomed to life on the prairie I loved Nature
with all my soul and saw in it all a manifestation of God's greatness, more plainly and more
elevating than it ever appeared to me in more
civilized surroundings.

The glow of daylight had just begun to penetrate in among the branches of the sycamores; there was dew on the willow leaves;
the aspect of everything far and near grew

clearer and clearer. On the opposite side of
the river the prairie hens began to stir,—little
gray things, black about the neck and with a
small tuft of feathers on the head. They bus-
ied themselves about the water's edge, thrust
down their bills and drank, skipped up and
down and prepared themselves for their day's
work.

"Oh, how good it is here!" whispered Lilian; and I myself thought what happiness it
would be to remain here in a small hut that I
had a right to call my own, with Lilian; to
spend all my days here, in her company, quietly and peacefully. It seemed to us both that
to the rich joy pervading all nature we had
added our own; that we had woven our own
peace of heart into that of our surroundings,
and that the gold of morning lay scattered
over it all,—over the pure joy we felt in our
hearts.

Soon there was seen a ring in the water's surface, suggestive of a movement below. And then there appeared a snout surrounded by whiskers and a moist, shining beaver's head, followed by another. Both animals swam in the direction of the house, cleaving the sparkling water before them. When they had reached their habitation, they climbed up on it, seated themselves on their hind legs and uttered a loud whine, whereupon, as though by magic, a number of other heads, larger and smaller, dove out of the sea. A general splash ensued. The little fellows joined the chorus of their two comrades and seemed to enjoy greatly to roam about the lake. But soon the first pair uttered a long, shrill tone, and in a moment the swarm divided into two troops, one of which took up their station at the dam, while the other disappeared among the willows on shore. There was a slight bustle all

around, and a sound of wood being fleezed,
or torn into shreds, which suggested that the
little animals had gone to work cutting down
what material was needed in their home-build-
ing.

For a long time we enjoyed watching the
occupation of the animals around us as it de-
veloped without disturbance on man's part.
Then Lilian, in changing her position, pushed
down the limb and a tree over which she was
leaning, and in the next minute the whole
picture was changed. The grating ceased, and
only a slight agitation of the water's surface
showed that something lay hidden at the bottom of the sea.   Soon the mirror was again
clear, and everything quiet.   The only sound
heard far and near was the hammering of a
woodpecker on one of the trunks of the sycamores.   The sun, however, rose higher and
higher; it grew quite warm; but as Lilian felt

strong enough we decided to walk around the river bend. We went along, but soon were confronted with a narrow creek that flowed through the forest and was emptied in the main stream. Lilian was unable to jump, and so, in spite of all protestations, I took her on my arm and carried her across. But the creek proved a source of great temptation, for in her fear of being dropped Lilian flung her arms about me and nestled her head on my shoulder, trying to hide her confusion. I paid no heed to this, however, but kissed her sweet lips again and again, and held her firmly in my arms. On reaching firm ground I hesitated in letting her down, but she tore herself away from me, and we both were possessed by a singular embarrassment. Lilian looked about uneasily, and the color came and went in her face. We walked on. I seized her hand and pressed it silently. The day grew

warmer and warmer; no wind moved among
the sycamores, and the foliage hung down
motionless, as if exhausted with heat and sunshine. I felt as if an air of witchcraft hung
over the forest, as if we two, Lilian and I, were
alone amidst a great enchantment. The girl,
however, grew more and more tired of walking; her breath became shorter and louder,
and her cheeks burned with heat. I asked if
she was tired and wanted to rest. "Oh, no,
no," she quickly replied, as if she herself had
thought of the same thing, but given it up
again. But in a few moments she tottered,
stopped and whispered:

"No, really I cannot walk further."

So I took her once more on my arm and
carried her down to the water, in among the
willow growth, which formed a dense roof
above, while beneath was a soft carpet of moss
and other vegetation. Here I laid her down,

kneeled by her side and was for awhile terribly frightened, as in fact every trace of color had left her face and her eyes wide open, in a sort of terror.

"Lilian, my dear child, I hope you are not sick," cried I. "Do you not know me? I am with you."

"Lilian," I continued, as she remained passive, "my beloved, my chosen one—my wife!"

At these words a tremor ran through her whole body; she threw her arms around me in a passionate, feverish manner, and whispered:

"My dear, my dear, my husband!"

And then I forgot everything about me, the glow of the sun, the heat, my tired feeling. I remember no longer how and when I awoke from this happy intoxication, but when at length I looked around, sunset lingered in the tree-tops. The woodpeckers were quiet, and

the setting sun was reflected in the water below, the inhabitants of the river had gone to
rest; around and above us rose the shadows
of the evening, as if dispelling the light that
was yet saturating the atmosphere all around.

It was time to return to camp.

As we stepped out of the thicket I turned
around and looked at Lilian. Her glance was
as mild and pure as before, full of love and
happiness. As I reached her my hand she
drew near and laid her head upon my shoulder, saying:

"Ralph, say once more that I am your wife,
and repeat it often to me."

And amidst the wilderness and under the
open sky I said to her:

"Here, in the presence of God and His
great works, in His name, I declare to you,
Lilian Morris, that I take you for my wife."

Whereat she replied:

"Yes, henceforth, and in all eternity, I am, and I remain, your wife, Ralph."

From this moment hence I looked at her, not as my friend and sweetheart, but as my lawful wife. And we both delighted in this thought. I felt elevated to a new trust, a new life, a new position in the world, the center and care of which was my respect for Lilian, which called forth every noble thought within me, appealing to my honor and becoming gradually one of life's greatest blessings. We returned to camp hand-in-hand. Our people had already become somewhat restless on account of our long absence. Some had even gone out in search of us, and I heard with much astonishment that several men had even passed by the beavers' lake and called my name, but without receiving a reply. In order to give room to no false impressions I called the expedition together, and when they had

10

formed a ring about us I took Lilian's hand
and said:

"Gentlemen, you are my witnesses that before you all I take this woman, who stands at
my side, for my lawful wife, and you will tes-
tify before the courts, before any judge and
anyone, wherever it may be, if you are called
upon, that such is the case."

"All right, and hurrah for you both!" cried
the men, whereupon old Smith, according to
the established custom of the country, inquired of Lilian if she agreed to have me for
her husband, and when she had given her
"yes," we were considered man and wife before the world.

On the great prairies of the West, and
wherever no towns exist, where there are no
jurisdiction and no churches, weddings were
in those days authorized in the manner described: all that was needed concentrated it-

self in the declaration that the contracting
parties wished to live beneath one roof and to
be considered rightfully husband and wife.
This was considered as binding as any judicial
document. None of my people considered my
marriage anything but binding on the basis
of what had taken place. Everyone viewed
the union kindly, for even though I had maintained a more strict discipline among them
than they had experienced from others, they
knew how good my intentions were on their
behalf, and proved from day to day that they
were much devoted to me. Lilian had been
their chosen favorite during the whole of our
journey, so it required but a short while to
call up a festive sentiment. Fires were kin-
dled; the Scotsmen produced their lutes,
played and sang; the Americans selected their
customary instruments, and so the evening
passed with music and festive shooting. Aunt

Atkins, now laughing, now crying, persisted in taking Lilian to her heart and maintained a constant skirmish with her pipe, which persistently refused to keep fire. Most of all, however, was I touched by a ceremony that corresponded so well with the easily moved sentiments of a class of people that is accustomed to move around a great deal in tented wagons. When the moon went down, the men seized some burning sticks from the fires and formed a procession headed by old Smith. They conducted us from one wagon to another, repeating the question, "Is this your home?"

My fair little wife answered "No," whereupon we went on. By Aunt Atkins's wagon some stir prevailed among the crowd, for this had hitherto served as Lilian's home during the journey. And great was the commotion when, after Lilian had answered her "No."

Aunt Atkins burst forth like a lioness, with something between a sob and a roar, and pressed Lilian to her heart, repeating over and over again:

"My little one, my sweet one!"

And when Lilian herself was carried away with the old woman's emotion, for a moment all these strong men became quite moved. Scarcely one eye remained without a tear. When we came up to my own wagon, it was found to be beautifully decorated with leaves and garlands of prairie flowers. Here the men raised their torches higher yet, and Smith asked in a louder and more earnest tone than before:

"Is this your home?"

"So it is, so it is," answered Lilian.

The men uncovered their heads, and it was quiet all around. Only the cracking of the torchwood was audible. Then the old. white-haired miner extended both his hands over us, saying:

"God's blessing upon both of you, and upon your home! Amen."

And when in a little while a loud hurrah, three times repeated, had closed the solemnity, they all retired and left myself and my wife alone together.

When they all had gone, Lilian nestled her head on my breast and whispered:

"Forever, forever!"

And our happiness rose higher than the stars above us, higher than anything visible from this earth of ours.

CHAPTER VI.

On the following morning, my wife being yet asleep, I left the wagon and went out in search of fresh flowers. While walking over the prairie I repeated again and again before myself: "You are married,"—and the thought filled my heart with a joy so great that I believed it would be right to thank God then and there, that he had permitted me to live long enough for realizing what it really means to be two in one; to see the world through the beloved one.

Now there was at least something in the world that I was permitted to call my own, and although what I could call "home" at present limited itself to a tented wagon I considered myself rich and happy in this posses-

sion, and regarded my lonely life of former
days with a feeling of pity,—my adventurous,
unbalanced bent of mind. I wondered how
such an existence was after all possible. Never
before had I been able to measure the depth
of the expression "your wife;"—to recognize
the fact that one called upon his own heart
in uttering these words, pronouncing the better part of his own self.

For some time I had loved Lilian dearly;
all the world centered in her, was attracted
and embodied in her. And now, calling her
my wife and reflecting upon her as mine own
for all time to come, it seemed that my happiness would certainly rob me of all my senses.
That I, a poor human creature, should be the
possessor of such a treasure! What else did
I require than this? Why, unless our destination had been safer and in many respects more
pleasant than where we were, and if not I had

been bound by duty; if not, indeed, I had been obliged to bring my people to the journey's end, I should gladly have relinquished all thoughts of California and taken up my residence, with Lilian, in Nebraska.

I went to California in pursuit of gold, but this purpose now seemed to me altogether ridiculous. What were all the earth's treasures to me, if I had her!

What use would we have for the possession of gold? If selecting for our homestead a place where there was eternal spring; if I felled some trees and built a hut, wielding my plough and my gun as best I knew, would this not protect us abundantly against all need?

Such were the thoughts that occupied me in my search of the prairie's wealth of vegetation. When I had gathered all I considered necessary, I returned to camp, and was met there by Aunt Atkins.

"Is the little one yet asleep?" inquired she, taking the indispensable pipe from her mouth in putting the question.

"Certainly," said I, "she is."

Whereupon she winked knowingly.

"Ah, you rascal!"

The little one, however, did not sleep yet, for we both saw her descending from the wagon, shade her eyes with her hand before the blazing sun and look around in all directions. Noticing me at a distance she came up, fair and blushing like the morning itself, and as I extended my arms toward her she flew into my embrace, offering me her mouth for a kiss.

"Good morning, good morning!" called I, in Polish.

She stood up on tiptoe, looked into my eyes and said in a roguish manner:

"Here is your wife."

On this announcement there followed sundry exchanges of endearments.

These happy days of rest and joy passed rapidly, without any abundance of work on my part, for old Smith had taken upon himself the leadership until the time came for departing. We paid one more visit to the beaver colony and crossed the river above it in a small canoe made of light wood and roughly hewn for pleasure trips up and down the stream. We went along the stream some distance and observed a herd of buffaloes tearing up the clayey soil with their horns, until their broad foreheads looked like covered by a thick-coated, protective armor of dry earth. Two days before the departure we put a stop to our excursions, as the Indians had shown themselves in the surrounding country, and, on the other hand, my wife was not quite well. She grew pale and seemed to

suffer, but answered, nevertheless, all ques-
tions regarding her ailment by stating that it
was nothing serious. I watched over her with
great care, both by day and during her sleep,
and at length was quite weak and tired with
trouble and waking. Aunt Atkins continued
winking her left eye in a provokingly knowing manner, whenever I mentioned Lilian's
sickness to her, and surrounded herself with
a cloud of smoke so thick that it certainly
would forever have enshrouded any man's
ordinary troubles. Mine, too, might have disappeared, if not Lilian had become possessed with a curious thoughtfulness. She
imagined that we perhaps sinned in loving
each other so much as we did, and one day
she even placed her finger at a certain verse
in the Bible, saying:

"Read this, Ralph!"

I followed her admonition and confessed to

be conscious of a certain embarrassing re
straint on seeing these words:

"Who changed the truth of God into a li*
and worshipped and served the creature more
than the Creator, who is blessed forever?"

As I read these words she said:

"If the Lord is angry with us I am sure that
I shall alone suffer the punishment it brings
upon us."

I did all I could to satisfy her that love was
a divine feeling, which elevates two human
souls when they are in unison, and makes
them thankful to the Creator. Through their
love they sing His praise.

Henceforth, however, there was no more
conversation of this kind between us. Wagons
and animals must be made ready for the continuation of our journey, and a thousand details in our preparations claimed my time and
my attention.

When at length we departed I could not
forbear shedding some tears in leaving the
place where we had enjoyed such happiness.
Besides, the sight of our caravan, once more
on the way, made me thoughtful of the great
responsibility I had assumed and anxious to
discharge my duties in this respect as faith-
fully as possible. Now every day would bring
us nearer to the end of our journey.

The beginning, however, was less auspi-
cious than we could desire. From the river
region to the foot of the Rocky Mountains
the land forms a long, even slope. The
draught animals were quickly exhausted and
would often stand still for a long time to
gather sufficient strength for the next strain.
Owing to the continuation of high water in
the Platte River this stream was useless to
us, and besides the hunting season had arrived, when Indians swarmed the plains in

search of the herds of buffaloes. Our night service grew long and tiresome; no day passed without the sign of alarm being given, and on the fourth day of our journey a detachment of redskins was caught in the very act of making a "stampede"—an attempt of bringing away our mules. One source of exasperation was the absence of camp fires occasioned by the want of fuel; for as we dared not approach the river, only a little brushwood here and there could be utilized, and even this was mostly soaked by the rain that poured down in streams from day to day.

The great herds of buffaloes which we constantly met gave me some alarm also. Often there would appear far off in the horizon large flocks of hundreds, or even thousands, of these animals, which galloped along like a hurricane, knocking down everything in their way. If such a flock would meet our caravan we should be hopelessly lost. Besides, the prairie was full of wild animals in pursuit of the buffaloes, for the latter do not only attract the Indians, but also the terrible grizzly bears and the gray wolves, which were abundant in Kansas and in the Indian Territory. About the little ponds and creeks where we pitched our camps for the night there would often be found a complete menagerie of wild beasts that came down to drink. Once one of the mestizoes was attacked by a bear, and unless old Smith, and Tom, another of our choice men, had come to poor Wichit's rescue, he would have been torn to pieces without fail.

I crushed the skull of the animal with so powerful a blow that the handle of my axe broke then and there. The beast, however, did not give out, until Smith and Tom had fired their guns into its ears. These fearful animals were so bold that during the night they would walk into our camp quite fearless. In one week we killed two of them scarcely a hundred yards from the wagons. At sunset the dogs would begin to howl so dismally that the night was unrestful to all of us.

In past days I had reveled in such a life as this, and only two years previous I roamed about the Arkansas wilderness amidst dangers much greater than these. At present, however, knowing that my wife, instead of sleeping, waked in fear and terror over my safety, suffering her health to be wasted, I wished the Indians, the bears and jaguars to Halifax and longed with all my soul to provide a place of rest and safety for that frail being whose welfare was most precious to me, of all things. My heart was unburdened, consequently, of no mean trouble, when at length we arrived, after three weeks' incessant wan-

11

derings, at a white stream called Republican
River, but whose waters, which looked as if
clogged with a chalk-like substance, were yet
carrying an English name. The broad, seam
dark rushes, which surrounded it, promised
for us an abundance of fire-materials, for although these rushes sputter a great deal and
send out an abundance of sparks, they burn
much better than moist wood. Here, then,
we allowed ourselves two days of rest. The
high bluffs which surrounded the water gave
promise of a difficulty in fording the stream
and served as an illustration of what difficulties we were destined to meet even before
reaching the immediate region of the Rocky
Mountains. As the place was quite far above
the sea level the cold at night made itself
rather keenly felt.

The difference in temperature by day and
by night gave us enough to do. Several of

our people, and old Smith among them, suffered with fever and were obliged to remain in their wagons. They appeared to carry within them yet the germ of the sickness first induced into their system at the unhealthy surroundings of the Missouri. Their sickness came at a most inopportune time. But as we had now arrived within a close proximity of the mountains, their complete recovery could be only a matter of time. My wife, too, was unwell, but I gave her every possible attention. She, however, seemed to suffer a great deal. Every morning, on wakening, I looked eagerly into her beautiful face; but my heart beat loud with uneasiness on account of the sickly paleness which overspread it, and of the dark rings around her eyes. It happened sometimes that she opened her eyes while I thus watched her, and closed them again with a smile. In such moments I would fain have given half of my own health to have landed safely with her in California.

But how far, how far we were as yet from the promised land! After two days' stopping we continued our journey and chose a way a little more southward, in order to follow the river's course as long as possible. The land —we were now within the borders of the State of Colorado—grew more and more mountainous; the river-bed lowered itself among high granite rocks, now single, now extending before us like compact walls, here in closed lines, there breaking out in promontories. Of firewood we had now sufficient for all our needs, as every fissure and gulch was closely beset with oaks and pines. Here and there a well penetrated with its clear water the impenetrable rocks. The air was cool, pure and invigorating; and in the course of one week the fever had completely left us.

Only the animals, which had no longer access
to such rich pastures as those in Iowa and
Nebraska, and to which the wild herds of the
mountain region offered no nourishment,
grew more and more emaciated under the
heavy burdens they were required to pull
along the acclivity.

At length we came in view one day of a
fantastic-looking mount looming up in the
horizon; ragged clouds surrounded its uppermost part; its summit was plunged into a
golden haze, which appeared to emanate from
it, spread itself over the earth and melted
away in the distant far-away.

Through the camp went a cry of joy; the
people climbed the wagons in order to obtain
a better view, and from all sides rose the cry,
"Rocky Mountains, Rocky Mountains!"
There was joy and hope in every one's eyes.

While my people greeted the mountains I

went into my wagon, pressed Lilian to my heart and promised her once more to remain true and faithful in all my dealings with her. In the presence of the great altar which stood erected before my eyes, and from which a mysterious, awe-inspiring influence appeared to emanate, we renewed our vow of remaining one together, until death should part us. When the sun went down and her shadows already spread themselves over the plains and promontories and the peaks far away, the latter looked like heads of giants overflown with gold. The ruddy glow soon died out, however, changing into a violet hue, which became darker and darker, until at length the darkness of night enveloped it all and one star after another peeped forth from behind the cloak thrown over the earth. We were yet about a hundred and fifty miles from the main part of the mountains, which during our

marches would occasionally disappear from
view altogether, but always loomed up whenever the weather became clear. We proceeded but slowly, as the road was full of obstacles; and although we pressed forward with
all our might, these would again and again
hinder our progress. Although carefully
guarding our strength against being over-
taxed we were constantly compelled to make
circuits and to halt while the road was being
explored. The ground bore only a scant vegetation of wild peas and gray mountain grass,
which offered no nourishment for the mules.
The long, tough runners, which grew out into
all directions and were intertangled in one
another, would often impede our progress
considerably. They wound themselves
around the horses' feet and the wheels of the
wagons, and often required considerable work
to be loosened and removed.

From time to time we stopped before gigantic fissures in the earth's crust, often several hundred yards wide, which had to be
evaded. Again and again Wichit and Tom,
our two pathfinders, returned with a report of
new impediments. One day it seemed as if
we were descending into a valley, when it
was discovered that the ground a little ahead
of us formed a precipitate plunge into a bot-
tomless gulch. We glanced in horror at the
mouth of the abyss, the precipitous rocks, the
vertical walls on the opposite side. Gigantic
oaks which grew in the depths below appeared like small herbs. Choosing another
way, we came farther and farther in among
the rocks, over natural bridges and past
chaotic masses of stone without definite shape.
The echo from the rocks doubled and re-
doubled the swearing and yelling of the drivers, as well as the plaintive braying of the

mules. Our wagons, which seemed so tall and monumental in the prairie, disappeared almost completely among the surrounding masses of stone and were scarcely visible down in the gulfs. The little cataracts, or, as the Indians name them, "the laughing waters," stopped our progress every few thousand feet. Our own resistance, as well as that of the animals, was rapidly exhausting, and yet the main chain, which had at first been visible in the horizon, had not drawn very much nearer. Happily our curiosity was yet greater than our exhaustion; the constantly changing scenery kept awake our spirits. None of my people, not even those born in the Allegheny region, had ever seen such wild landscapes. Even I myself regarded in wonder this world of rocks, which our imagination would shape into the queerest architectoric formations. From time to time we were met

by Indians belonging to tribes different from
those of the prairie. They were less numerous than those, but wilder. The sight of the
Whites roused their savage instinct of blood-
shed. Their appearance was more repulsive
even than that of their Nebraska brethren.
Of taller stature and darker hue, as they were,
their everted nostrils and unsteady glance
gave them a resemblance of wild beasts. In
speaking they touched their cheeks with their
thumbs. Their war paint was rich and elab-
orate, their armature consisted of bows and
arrows made of a kind of hard wood so strong
that our people could not use them at all. In
large numbers these men might have been
quite dangerous, as their principal characters
appeared to be a desire of unlimited rapa-
ciousness. Happily, however, their number
was limited, and we never saw at one time
more than some fifteen of them. They were

called "Yampos." Their language was not
even understood by Wichit, our mestizo,
though he was well versed in all Indian dia-
lects. We therefore never comprehended why
they all pointed first at the Rockies, then at us,
opened and shut their hands and appeared
desirous of imparting to us some information.

The difficulties continued so that our progress scarcely exceeded fifteen miles each day.
The horses, being less powerful than the
mules and less adaptable to all kinds of food,
began falling. Even the men began to show
signs of exhaustion, having been obliged
sometimes to pull with the mules, wherever
these could not alone force their way. A tired
and impatient mood seized the weaker ones,
and one, who, owing to over-exertion, had
had a fit of hemorrhage, died on the way,
cursing the hour when he had resolved upon
leaving the safety of his New York home.

We really had reached the worst part of the way, namely the country surrounding a small creek named Kiow by the Indians. Here was not such an abundance of rough rocks as are found in Eastern Colorado, but the whole region was so densely strewn with large and small stones that it was extremely difficult to pass along with the wagons. These fragments of rocks, here standing upright, there thrown out over the ground in a chaotic confusion, conveyed the impression of a gigantic church-yard. We had indeed reached the "bad lands" of Colorado, which correspond to a barren stretch of country running through the northern part of Nebraska. Summoning all our strength, we succeeded in covering this part of the journey in the course of one week.

CHAPTER VII.

Our next halt was not made until we had reached the foot of the Rocky Mountains.

I could not conceal a feeling of unrest on finding myself face to face with this region of gigantic rocks and mountains which hid their summits in the clouds, extending as far as the view would pass and shrouding themselves in a distant, misty haze. The quiet majesty and sublimity of the view oppressed me; I bowed down before the Creator and asked him to lend me His help and guidance in bringing our people and our property safely across these walls of solid stone. I asked Him also to protect my wife against the danger that threatened us beneath these masses of impenetrable rocks. And so we walked

forward into this world of mountains; and
the doors of the world closed upon us. Above
us were seams of rocks and some vultures cir-
cling about in the air, but nothing else. We
walked amidst a perfect labyrinth of paths,
rocks, beneath towering domes, past gulches,
cracks, caves and holes, surrounded by gigantic rooms where a perfect quiet reigned. It
was so solemn and imposing, and even the
soul seemed enclosed within a stone enclosure
so completely that even man himself became
frightened at his own voice and, not daring
to speak aloud, communicated his thoughts in
a whisper. It seemed that the road was continually closing in upon us; as if a voice whispered into our ear: "Go back, go back; you
shall come no farther than this!"—as if we
were attempting to penetrate into some deep
mystery that the Creator himself had sealed.
When at night these gigantic rocks loomed

up around us and the moon's white glare
made deep shadows among the stones; when
the "laughing water" assumed magic shapes,
even the most hardened adventurer felt the
spell of the surroundings. We sat for hours
by the fire, glancing in fear and superstition
down into the dark gulches, almost expecting
something terrible to come into appearance
from down there. One day we found in a
depression between two rocks a human skeleton, with some hair yet adhering, and though
some weapons that lay near by signified that
the body was that of an Indian, yet we all felt
a premonition of something fearful. This
skeleton, with its grinning rows of teeth,
seemed to imply that here was no way out.
On the same day Tom, one of the mestizoes,
met his death, falling down a precipice with
his horse. A deep sorrow filled our hearts.
Hitherto our progress had been made in a

hopeful, glad spirit; even the drivers had
ceased swearing. Now the caravan wound
its way along the barren ground in silence.
The mules became, however, more and more
ungovernable; if one pair stood still all those
following were obliged to do the same. One
of my greatest cares was that in these days
of trouble and constant excitement I was unable to remain by my wife, who needed my
help so greatly. I was obliged, however, to
set a good example before my companions,
and to inspire into them fresh courage and
vigor. The people bore their burden, however, with that patience which distinguishes
the Americans, but in reality their strength
would no longer prevail against the strain to
which they were exposed. My own health,
however, withstood it all, although there were
many nights when I enjoyed only a couple of
hours' rest. I pulled the wagons like the

others, took my turns among the watchmen,
walked about the camp,—in one word, I tried
to fill my place not only as the leader, but
also as a member of the expedition. It gave
me a great satisfaction to perform this service.
When I returned to my wagon, tired and exhausted, I found there the woman for whose
sake I did it all, and who was herself the
choicest of the charges I had assumed,—whose
true heart and willing hand were the real
treasures I possessed on earth. Lilian, though
herself suffering from the hardship she was
obliged to share with the rest of us, would
never go to rest until I returned home, and
when I remonstrated with her she closed my
mouth with a kiss, asking me not to be angry.
She held my hand while sleeping, awoke often
and covered me from time to time with beaver
skin in order that I should not be exposed to
the cool air. Always tender, good and kind,

12

she was ever careful of my welfare. What
wonder, then, that I adored her; that her
whole being was sacred to me; that our
wagon seemed to me like a church. Though
in the presence of the colossal stone pillars
she appeared smaller than ever, she never disappeared before my view, even though I often
lost sight of the others.

After three weeks' incessant climbing we
finally reached open land and approached the
White River.   On entering this region we
were assaulted by a band of Indians belonging
to the Yutah tribe, which occasioned some
confusion among us, and gave me some con-
cern, as their arrows penetrated the roof of
my wife's wagon. We, however, routed them
so completely that three-fourths of their number remained on the spot, while the rest fled.
Only one prisoner was made, a boy of sixteen,
who, when reassured that no harm would be-

fall him, made the same gestures before us as
we had seen among the Indians at the other
side of the mountains, pointing now toward
the south, now toward us. He seemed to
indicate that there were white men not far
away, but this we could not credit. It was
true, nevertheless, and you may imagine our
surprise and joy when, on the second day
after reaching the plateau, we looked down
upon a broad valley and saw not only a number of wagons like our own, but moreover a
circle of newly-made huts surrounding a large
structure without windows. The valley was
traversed lengthwise by a river. A great
many mules grazed in the pastures and were
under guard of a number of riders. The presence of men of our own race caused me no
little astonishment, which, however, turned
into genuine fear when I reflected that these
supposed colonists might be outlaws who,

evading justice, had fled to the prairie and thence found their way across the mountains. I knew from personal experience that these persons, who considered themselves bound by no regard to society, would occasionally repair to a distant place, organize themselves in a military manner and resist any one that might attempt to bring them back to justice. Occasionally they would make an assault upon some peaceful colony and, being recruited from far and near, form a well-established colony somewhere in the wilderness. I had often met large numbers of outlaws west of the Mississippi at the time when I engaged in flooding timber down that great river. Occasionally these meetings had resulted in a bloody skirmish, during which I had had ample opportunity to witness their ability in handling arms of all kinds and their cruelty.

If Lilian had not been there I should have entertained no fear whatever; but the thought of the dangerous position in which she would be placed if we lost the fight, or even if I were killed, governed all other reflection. I, the fearless one, trembled like a common poltroon at the mere prospect of meeting a band of outlaws. If they were such, however, there would hardly be any chance to avoid hard fighting,—a fight that must be conducted on a plan quite different from the one we had adopted against the Indians.

I notified my people of the situation without delay, and told them to be ready for a desperate encounter. I tried to prepare myself for being killed or levelling the hornet's nest down below with the ground. It was my purpose to let the attack be made by ourselves. But in the meantime we had been observed, and two riders came toward us in full gallop. I breathed now a little more freely; the outlaws would have sent no delegation to meet us. We found that the colony was inhabited by trappers and hunters engaged by a fur trader's company, and who had made their "summer camp" at this place. Instead of engaging in a fight we were received most cordially, and received every attention needed from these rough-and-ready, but honest and kind-hearted prairie hunters. We thanked God for having an opportunity to enjoy such sweet rest. Two months and two weeks had passed since we left the banks of the Big Blue River; consequently our strength had nearly given out, and the mules were half dead. In complete safety and amidst pleasant surroundings we now ate, drank, rested, provided food for our animals during one whole week's time.

It all was to us almost the same as a de-

livery from a great danger. The chief of the
camp, a gentleman by the name of Thurston,
well educated and experienced, received me
very friendlily, having convinced himself that
we were a little better than common adventurers, and offered his own little house as an
abode for me and Lilian, whose health was by
no means as completely restored as I should
have liked to see.

For two days she remained in bed. She
was so completely exhausted that during the
first four and twenty hours she slept undis-
turbed, scarcely opening her eyes during all
that time. I watched by her bedside in order
to insure for her the necessary quiet, and was
content to sit for hours watching her repose.
After two days she was strong enough, however, to arise and walk about outside; but I
protested against her doing any kind of work.
Many of my people, too, were asleep for sev-

eral consecutive days, and when this was over
they began to repair the wagons and wash
their clothes. The brave hunters gave us a
most liberal assistance. They were mostly
Canadians and served the company, which
engaged them, during the whole year. They
spent the winter hunting beavers and big
game, and during the summer they assembled
in camp, preparing their spoils, which were
afterward sent across the country under safe
guard, for delivery. The service of these men,
who were usually engaged for a period of several years, was by no means easy. They were
forced to live in the most distant, abandoned
parts of the country, where, though there was
no want of game, their lives were always in
danger, as the Indians could never forgive
them for entering their territories. It is true
that their wages were high, yet most of them
cared little for the money, but enjoyed life in

the open country,—a life that but seldom terminated in a quiet old age.

The party was made up of men well prepared for their work, vigorous, healthy, capable of braving almost any danger. The appearance of these giants with their fur caps and long rifles always reminded me of Cooper's tales, which I had read in Boston. I regarded their camp and all their doings with no little interest.

They were organized on the strictest plan and with almost knightly rules of order. Thurston, who was their leader and the company's general agent, maintained a perfect military order among them. Every one was fearless, kind and good-hearted; the time we spent among them brought all of us genuine pleasure. Our own expedition, too, was viewed by them with favor, and they often repeated that a caravan so well provided was

hardly ever seen. Above all, my plan of
choosing a northern road instead of the southern one through St. Louis was pleasing to
Thurston. He told us that one expedition
of three hundred men under the command of
one Markwood, which had followed the southern route, suffered so much by heat that their
draught animals were all lost. Finally, they
were completely annihilated by the Indians.
The latter were then attacked by the Cana-
dian hunters, who killed a number of them
and took from them over one hundred scalps,
including that of Markwood.

This report made a great impression upon
my people, and even old Smith, who was not
the least brave of them, and who had at
first opposed my plan of going through
Nebraska, declared that I was more "smart"
than he, and that one might well bow
before my judgment. During the week

of rest, we all regained most of our lost strength.

Besides Thurston, with whom I established a firm bond of friendship, I became acquainted with a man well known in those days throughout the States, namely, "Mick," who did not belong to the party, but roamed about the prairies and mountains in the company of two other adventurers. These remarkable men went into genuine battles with large detachments of Indians, and their strength and ability made them throughout victorious. "Mick," of whom already many a book has been written, was viewed with such terror by the Indians that a word from him counted even more than a whole delegation from the Government could do. The Government therefore often made use of his service in treating with the redskins, and subsequently he was elected governor of Oregon.

At the time when I made his acquaintance he
was fifty years old, yet his hair was perfectly
black, and his glance bespoke kindness,
strength and great endurance. He was considered one of the strongest men in the United
States, and wrestling formed a part of our
amusements during our period of rest. He
was much interested in Lilian, to whom he
presented, on our departure, a pair of beautiful small moccasins, which he had made
with his own hands. This gift was gratefully
welcomed, for in truth my wife had worn out
all the footwear with which she had equipped
herself before starting.

At length we continued our journey under
the most favorable auspices, the road having
been described minutely to us, and it having
been explained what places we were to seek
and what to avoid. We carried with us a
good supply of salted meat, and in addition

Thurston had, in his great kindness, given us a number of strong mules in exchange for some of our own weakened ones. Mick, who had been in California, gave us a description of the wonderful climate prevailing there throughout the year, the wealth of the country, the magnificent forests and remarkable mountain regions, all of which were to be found nowhere else in the United States. Full of new hope and strength we started anew, not knowing what suffering we were destined to meet before the promised land could be reached.

We were loath to depart from the brave Canadians. The day of our departure will indeed be fixed in my remembrance as long as I live, for my beloved wife flung her arms around me and, while her color came and went, confessed in a whisper the news that

filled my heart with great joy and pride, namely, that I was no longer her husband alone,
but that I adored in her the mother of my
child.

CHAPTER VIII.

After two weeks' journey we reached the borders of Utah, and although the road was in the main quite tolerable, we proceeded more rapidly in the beginning than later on. Before us lay yet the western range of the mountains, a net of chains and highlands traversed by the Green and the Grand Rivers, two streams from which the great Colorado River receives its main tribute of water. The numerous creeks which emanate from the highlands afford a number of comparatively quiet, comfortable passes. So we reached without difficulty Lake Utah, where the salt steppes begin. We were surrounded by a singular landscape of uniform character; wide plains ascending in terraces of highland and smaller peaks flanked by towering masses of stone; all this succeeded itself in tiresome sameness. These regions are stamped with such an air of severity, loneliness and death that the heart quails beneath the sight thereof. Here are the salt lakes with their barren surroundings.

Far and wide was not a single tree, no vegetation, indeed, of any kind. The soil is covered with a crust of salt, in which no vegetation lives, save some grayish shrubs with thick leaves containing a watery juice saturated with salt.

The wanderings in these regions are exceedingly tiresome, as one may continue onward for weeks through the same barren desert, always surrounded by the same uniform mountains and the endless steppes. Once more our strength threatened to give out. In the open prairie we had felt some loneliness, but this was the loneliness of death itself.

Little by little most of us surrendered to a feeling of general indifference. We crossed the western borders of Utah; still the same dead soil! We passed into Nevada, and things remained the same. The sun was so hot that our heads threatened to burst; and the reflection from the ground hurt our eyes. The air was filled by a fine dust the origin of which we were unable to trace, but which made the eyelids quite sore. Sometimes one or more of the mules would fall down, as if suddenly stunned and blinded.

The majority of our people retained their good hopes, believing that hardly more than one or two weeks would pass when we should reach the Sierra Nevada, and beyond, the beautiful land of California. Days and months passed, however, and our sufferings grew

13

more and more intense. In one week alone
we were obliged to abandon three of our
wagons, as the mules could no longer draw
them forward. This was indeed a land of
misery and hopelessness. In Nevada the desert grew more and more barren, and before
long sickness was added to our long list of
calamities.

One morning old Smith was reported sick,
and I found to my consternation that he had
contracted typhus fever. One cannot with
impunity pass from one climate into another.
The short periods of rest cannot eliminate the
exhaustion altogether, and amidst hardships
and inadequate nutrition the disease germs
develop most rapidly. Lilian at once took up
her station by Smith's couch and devoted all
her attention to the man who had been the
sponsor of our bond and blessed us as a father.
I trembled for her fate, but had no right to

prevent her in discharging her duty as a Christian. So, with both of the aunts, she spent day and night at the sick man's bedside, without a murmur on my part.

On the second day he lost consciousness; on the eighth he expired in Lilian's arms. We buried him, and many were the tears that fell upon the grave of this man, who had been my best helpmate, my true and fatherly friend and companion. We hoped that after this painful sacrifice God would have pity upon us; but this was only the beginning of our afflictions, for on the very same day another man became sick, and during the days following there was a patient in nearly every wagon. We continued our journey, hoping against hope; and the sickness constantly craved its tribute of health and life. Aunt Atkins, too, was unwell, but thanks to Lilian's indefatigable care recuperated quickly. My heart be-

came almost cold with fear whenever I saw
Lilian bending over the couches. Often, while
performing a sentinel's duty at the edge of
our camping grounds, I took my head in both
my hands, scarcely knowing what to do. I
poured out my heart before God in warm
appeals to His mercy; I prayed that He would
spare my wife's life, but was hardly able to say
truthfully: "Lord, Thy will be done, and not
mine!"

Even at night, when we were together, I
fancied that a ghost was looking into our
wagon, in search of Lilian. Every moment
I did not spend in her company was full of
pain and apprehension to me. Hitherto, however, Lilian had been as well as was possible
under the circumstances. The strongest persons fell down exhausted, but she went about
her duties, though pale and thin, but comparatively healthy. I hardly dared to inquire

about her condition, but took her in my arms
without a word. When I wanted to speak, a
fear indefinable, but sufficient to quail my
heart, lamed my very faculty of speech.

We were now nearing the western part of
Nevada, where the salt steppes and mountains
are succeeded by an even, fertile prairie.
When for two days the sickness ceased among
us I hoped that our misery would be at an
end. Indeed, it was time that it might.

Nine of our people had succumbed, six
more were unable to rise. Our strict main-
tenance of rule and order had relaxed under
these conditions. The horses were almost all
lost; the mules had long been reduced to
mere skin and bone. Of the fifty wagons that
had left the friendly camp of the hunters, now
only thirty-two were dragged through the
desert. We had taken no precaution to keep
up our provisions, as no one dared, for fear

of being attacked by sickness in a lonely place, to go hunting the game that was observed at long intervals. For over a week we fed upon black earth squirrels, fearing that our provisions would come to a premature end, though the evil-smelling meat of these animals could hardly be swallowed by any one of us. But even this poor source of food was present in but scant measure. Immediately on reaching the water beyond, we would find big game in abundance.

We again encountered the Indians, who, according to their custom, attacked us early in the morning. One of their detachments, being supplied with shotguns, killed four of our men. In a hand-to-hand fight I was struck in the head by a tomahawk with such a force that I lost consciousness later in the day. Yet this was to me almost a happy incident, as Lilian was now attending me instead of paying attention to such patients as might, through their sickness, imperil her health. For three days I was confined to my wagon, and blessed were these days, when Lilian remained by me, changing the compresses with her nimble hands. When somewhat rested and once more able to move about I returned to my duties and convinced myself that I must not remain on the sick list when so much depended upon our progress.

Never before had I felt exhausted to such a great extent, and never had a few days' rest done me so much good before. The fear of my wife's fate, which constantly haunted me, was almost forgotten when I saw with what tenderness she watched me. When I moved about once more, there was no doubt in my mind, however, that it had now become an urgent necessity to press forward with as much speed as possible. The last horse was yet dragging itself along with much difficulty, had now become my only riding animal. So I made an effort to proceed with the greatest possible speed; but the difficulties increased from day to day. The heat successively became quite unnatural, and through the air drifted a dirty fog, like smoke from a distant fire. The horizon faded out, and the view was obscured all around; the sun's rays appeared pale and ruddy. The animals became uneasy; they ground their teeth and breathed with difficulty, as if they felt something disagreeable in the air. I considered it all due to the hot wind that blew across the land from the heated desert, but was obliged to abandon this theory as the air did not stir, and no straw was moving anywhere. The sun went down in a ruddy glare; the night was oppressively warm. The sick called for water, the dogs barked; I myself rode about the camp wondering if in the neighborhood there might be a prairie fire. Nowhere, however, could I see any indication of a fire.

I set my mind at rest thinking that a prairie fire must have taken place somewhere, but was in some way extinguished. On the day following we wondered at the numbers of rabbits, antelopes, buffaloes and squirrels that passed us, all going into an easterly direction, as though they fled out of that same California which we were so anxious to reach. As, however, the air became purer and the heat less oppressive, I decided that a prairie fire had really taken place west of us, but was now over, and that the animals sought fresh grazing places. It was necessary, then, to press forward as speedily as possible to see if the burned district could be passed by us, or if we would be required to make a circuit. I calculated that we could be no farther than three hundred miles from the Sierra Nevada. This meant some twenty days' journey, so I determined that every effort should be made to reach this destination. So we kept up our marches at night, as the noon sun exhausted the animals almost beyond repair, and they would always find some shadow among the wagons, where they could rest in the daytime.

One night, when I was sitting on horse-back, tired and thoughtful, we suddenly heard a singular crackling under the wheels of the wagons and the horses' hoofs. A cry of stop went through the whole caravan. I jumped off and saw that all the drivers had dismounted also. They were examining the ground about us, and at length one of them, whom I approached with an inquiry, looked up, saying:

"Captain, we are moving across the burned region."

On close examination I found indeed that the prairie beneath our feet was scorched along the earth's crust.

I ordered the caravan to stop, and we passed the night on this very spot. At sunrise a singular panoroma was unfolded before our eyes. As far as we could see nothing but a naked, black stretch of land was visible. The soil seemed covered with a glassy substance. We could not ascertain how far the burned region extended, as the horizon was yet darkened by clouds of smoke, but I turned toward the south, hoping to reach the place where the fire had started. What a journey across the burned prairie meant, this I knew from experience, having witnessed before how the animals died one by one from want of food. Judging from the wind's direction the fire had extended northward, by going in a southern direction I hoped, then, to reach the edge of the burned district. The men obeyed my instructions, but with some hesitation, as we were entering upon a new part of our journey and being liable to suffer a delay, God knew how long. At noon the horizon cleared up, however, but the heat was so intensified that one felt almost as if the atmosphere itself was on fire. Then something wonderful occurred.

Quite unexpectedly the horizon became perfectly clear, and far away lay the green, smiling, sunlit heights of the Sierra Nevada. The peaks were covered with snow, but the slopes and the dark green forests suggested a welcome rest. It seemed as if the fresh breeze from the mountains could already be felt; as if we already smelled the odor of the pine wood, and that only a few hours' march would bring us to the flowery slopes. Our men at once forgot their tiredness, the uni-

formity of the desolate plains around us and
our past suffering. Some nearly lost their reason for joy. Others threw themselves on the
ground, sobbing aloud, or lifted their arms
toward the sky and cried out in ecstasy.
Lilian and I both laughed and wept for joy,
and my astonishment was great, as I thought
we were at least a hundred and fifty miles from
California. Instead of this, however, the
mountains smiled at us beyond the sooty soil,
beckoning us to approach. Although the
time reserved for our rest had not yet elapsed,
the people would hear of nothing but proceed
at once. Even the sick ones folded their hands
and begged that we would continue our journey at once. So we went on, and the cracking
of the embers, the drivers' shouts, their rapid
movement and joyous calls made a new and
unwonted spectacle. No more was said of
going around the burned region.

And what use would it indeed have been
to make a long circuit, when only a small
number of miles separated us from our destination!

Before very long, however, the view of the
mountains was enshrouded in the scene of
the burning or burned prairie. Hours passed;
the horizon grew narrower and narrower;
night came, and we proceeded on our way beneath the starlit sky. The mountains were
evidently farther off than we at first thought.

Near midnight the mules began to show
signs of desperation, so the caravan stopped.
The animals fell down exhausted. In vain
it was tried to bring them on their feet. No
one closed his eyes this night. At dawn we
looked eagerly after the sunny slopes, but
nothing save the former dismal view was visible. As far as the eye could reach there was
nothing but the same dreary stretch of land;

the same narrow horizon. Of the mountains not a trace was visible.

My people stood like petrified, but I thought of the ominous mirages that often occur in such places. Now it was all clear. A feeling of indefinite horror crept over me. What was now to be done? Continue in the same direction? Or turn back? And where were the borders of the burned district? Would the strength of the mules prevail? Indeed, I hardly dared to measure the depth of the gulf which extended before us.

In order to know what were our immediate prospects I ascended one of the nearest hills from where I commanded a larger view of the prairie than otherwise. Through the telescope I discovered something green far away, but when we drew nearer it was found to be one of the many ponds where the fire had not been able to scorch the vegetation. Nowhere could we detect a single trace of life. It was now clear to me that we must retrace our steps until we reached fertile grounds.

But my orders were no longer obeyed. The men drove on, answering all remonstrance on my part by repeating:

"There are the mountains; there we want to go."

I ventured no direct opposition, seeing that no human power would have prevailed against the men's determination.

Perhaps I thought of returning with Lilian, but my wagon had been left behind, and Lilian occupied Aunt Atkins's wagon.

So we pursued our way. Once more night surrounded us, and with it a deep quiet. The moon rose fiery red over the black, naked soil. In the morning only one-half of the number of mules was yet moving, the remainder having fallen on the way. The heat became so intense that everything seemed like molten fire. One of the patients died in violent cramps, and no one collected himself sufficiently to bury the body. We plodded on, as best we could. A pool similar to the one we had found on the day previous kept us alive and reinvigorated man and beast alike for a while, but without adding to our strength. For thirtysix hours the mules had had no feed. We gave them what little there was left of straw in the wagons, but even this was quite insufficient.

As our way was now continuously dotted with dead animals, on the third day we had only one animal, which I claimed for Lilian's use. The wagons, which contained all the utensils we should need for earning our bread in California, were left behind in the desert. Soon the worst of all plagues, namely, hunger, made itself felt among us. A great deal of victuals had been left behind with the wagons,

14

and all we possessed was what each one ot us had strength enough to carry with him. Far and wide we saw no sign of life. I had yet a little biscuit and a piece of salt meat, but kept it for Lilian, and could not persuade myself to touch it. And the desert seemed yet endless.

To increase our suffering the mirage of the mountains was seen again in broad daylight. But the nights were terrible. All the sun-rays that were absorbed by the earth in the daytime were again eradicated at night, scorching the soles of our feet and drying our throats in a most exasperating manner. In such a night one of our men became insane. He sat down on the ground, rocking to and fro and laughing in a frenzied manner. When the mule that carried Lilian fell, it was at once surrounded by two hundred hungry men, who literally tore it to pieces. Two more days passed, and the people looked like maniacs. Some even began to threaten one another. They knew that we had no more food, but also that whoever demanded anything of one would be a dead man in the next second, so their self-preservation was yet able to keep in check their animal instincts. I gave what little I had to Lilian in the night, in order not to excite the desperation of the men by producing my little store of victuals in their presence. Lilian besought me to share her ration, but I told her she would see me dead first. Yet, in spite of my watchfulness, she succeeded in reserving a few bites for Aunt Atkins and Aunt Grosvenor. I myself felt constantly the pain of hunger. My old wounds burned. For five days I had had no food save the water we drank at the last pool on our way. The thought that there was bread and meat in my pocket, while still I dared not eat, nearly made me insane. I feared to lose consciousness, if my wounds broke up.

"Oh, God!" cried I, in my wretchedness, "do not deprive me of my reason. Do not allow me to lay my hands on what I have reserved for my wife!"

But God had no pity upon me. On the morning of the sixth day I saw some bright red spots in Lilian's face; her hands trembled, and she breathed with difficulty. She looked at me in agony and said:

"Ralph, you must save your own life and leave me behind. There is no hope for me."

I bit my lip to suppress the oath I would otherwise have uttered. Without a word of reply I pressed her to my heart. The fever burned in our eyes and veins.

And then I carried her along the desert. How I gathered the necessary strength I do not know. I felt neither pain nor hunger; I saw nothing but her and heeded nothing but her alone. In the night her condition grew worse, and she lay panting on the ground.

"Water, Ralph; water!"

My heart shrank with remorse; all I had was a particle of meat and some bread. In my desperation I cut into my hand with a knife and moistened her lips with my blood. But she cried out in terror and fainted by my side. Recovering in a little while she whispered:

"Do not be angry, Ralph,—I am your wife!"

I carried her along, but was on the seventh day almost beside myself with pain. The Sierra Nevada now really appeared in the horizon, but my wife died slowly in my arms. When the agony of the last moments came, I laid her on the ground and kneeled by her. Her eyes sought mine; one brief moment consciousness lighted up her glance, and she whispered:

"My dear, my husband!"

A tremor seized her, and there was a fear in her glance,—and then she passed away.

I tore the compress from my head, lost what consciousness was left within me, and did not know what followed. Like in a dream I felt that the men surrounded me, took away my weapons,—and—and dug a grave in the sod. Within me sounded the words:

"He who adores creation more than the Creator and serves it more than he serves the Creator — — —!"

One month after I regained the use of my senses. I had landed in the house of a Californian settler by the name of Moszynski. When my health was fully restored I returned to Nevada. An abundant vegetation of grass covered the prairie once more and spread its richness so completely over the ground that I could never hope to find the remains of my beloved wife. What I had done to call down upon me the Lord's vengeance so completely I do not know.

If at least I had been able to cry out my sorrow over my wife's grave, life would have been easier to live. But every year I search the Nevada plains, and every year in vain.

Years have now passed since those terrible days. And my lips have often repeated the words, Thy will be done. But I am lonely in the world without her. I move about, a man among men, laughing and smiling like the rest; but the heart has its own sorrows, its own loneliness, its lost love and secret thoughts to dwell upon — —.

I have grown old, and soon I shall face

Eternity.   Now I only hope that God will allow me to find there that heavenly image of my wife which was in part revealed to me on earth.

THE END.